NIKKI WEST

Be Mine Again

Contents

One

Chapter 1

Philip Brownsville remained close to the grave site and attempted to focus on the clergyman's words. Who was he joking? He simply maintained that this day should be finished. He felt like a charlatan. He hadn't arrived to offer his final appreciation to Peter Brownsville. He was here to ensure that the bastard was covered.

He wasn't amazed to see such countless individuals at the memorial service. He realized they weren't here for Peter. They were hanging around for him. Despite the fact that this was whenever he'd first come back in the neighborhood since…the "episode." Jesus. That appeared to be a lifetime back rather than a simple seven years. A great deal had changed from that point forward. He had changed. He expected the better.

His eyes filtered the little group, unknowingly looking for

Hannah. Presently, why on earth could Hannah be here today? After the manner in which you left Honey Springs a long time back? She's presumably hitched with a brood of children at this point.

His thoughts were interfered with by the Reverend Sutton's end invocation, "May you be calm and liberated from misery. May you discover a sense of harmony in death you were unable to track down throughout everyday life. So be it."

Mack took a full breath and gone to the reverend. "Much thanks to you for all you've done for the current week to get Peter in the ground."

"It was my pleasure to help out." He stopped briefly, as though uncertain how to proceed. "You know, Mack, I'm dependably accessible to talk. I know you and your dad were alienated these beyond couple of years — "

Philip's sharp dismiss cut his words. "Alienated. That is a decent word for it."

Reverend Sutton grinned generous and proceeded, "However on the off chance that you might want to discuss your sentiments, my entryway is dependably open."

Philip shook his head and said, "That's what I value, Reverend Sutton. Yet, the main inclination I have about Peter's passing is alleviation."

"Indeed, assuming things change, I'll be here."

Philip gestured courteously, then, at that point, looked to one side and froze. Hannah Everett. Their eyes met and everything around him disappeared. 1,000,000 contemplation went through his mind, and every one of them were advising him to let her be. He didn't tune in.

Susan Couldn't take her eyes off peter. It had been seven long years since she'd seen him. He'd been attractive as a young person. Be that as it may, presently? Presently he was stunning. His dull hair was short and there was a smidgen of five-o'clock shadow all over despite the fact that it was early evening. He wore a white dress shirt with the sleeves moved up and dim pants that fit his hips and legs perfectly. Her mouth went dry.

She'd showed up later than expected for the memorial service. For the most part since she'd contended with herself the entire morning about whether she ought to come. Her Southern habits prevailed upon pride and she arrived straightaway. She kept a decent distance since she'd showed up later than expected and in light of the fact that she didn't know she believed Mack should see her. Not that he'd mind somehow.

Philip hadn't come back to Honey Springs by any means in seven years. During that time, he hadn't called. Or on the other hand composed. Not once. For hell's sake, he hadn't even expressed farewell before he'd left. That had harmed the most. Clearly, the main explanation he'd return currently was to cover his dad.

To say that Peter Brownsville hadn't been a decent man was all in all a misrepresentation of the truth, however there was as yet a good assembling at his memorial service. Honey Springs may be little in size, yet it was enormous in heart. They weren't there for Peter. They were there for Philip .

The help was finished and individuals were withdrawing. Susan advised herself to leave immediately, before Philip saw her, yet she delayed. Her eyes went to Mack for another look since she'd likely at no point ever see him in the future. He was conversing with the clergyman. Recollections of the last time they were together hurried through her, and she was incapacitated with feelings she was unable to try and start to distinguish. Jesus, Susan. Take care of business. Simply go as of now. In any case, it was past the point of no return. Their eyes met. Her expectation that he wouldn't perceive her blurred as she watched him stroll toward her.

She chomped her lip and really mulled over making a run for her vehicle. For what reason would it be advisable for me to take off? I did nothing off-base. I'm not the person who vanished in that frame of mind of the night without a word to anybody. She fixed her back, raised her jawline high and tranquilly paused.

Then he was there. Directly before her and close enough to contact. Gracious god. He looked surprisingly better into close.

Briefly, the two of them just gazed at one another.

Philip gulped and said, "Susan."

Hannah made a sound as if to speak and said, "Philip. Please accept my apologies for your misfortune." She would have rather not taken a gander at him any longer. It hurt excessively, so she kept her look prepared on his shoulder.

"I was trusting that perhaps we could get together later and talk?" he asked hopefully.

Her eyes snapped to his. "Please accept my apologies. I don't believe that is smart." She upheld a couple of steps away and said, "It was decent seeing you once more, Philip." She turned and strolled smoothly to her vehicle, feeling his eyes on her the whole way.

Philip watched Susan leave. He had no real option except to let her go. He'd realized there was the chance he'd run into her while he was visiting the area. Yet, that hadn't set him up for his response to her. She'd been alluring quite a while back. In any case, presently? She was a knockout. She actually wore her hair in a similar short, pixie style. Yet, that charming little head was presently sitting on top of a lady's body. An experienced, delicious lady's body.

He hadn't seen a ring on her finger, however that didn't be guaranteed to mean she was single. He could ask around and — For what reason could you do that when you're simply going to be here a couple of additional days? She's from quite a while ago. Leave her there. You've made a decent life for yourself in Houston, including a well deserved advancement to investigator with the Houston Police Division. That is where your future is. Recall that.

"Philip, seeing you is great."

Philip turned away from watching Susan drive off and perceived Charlie Weaver, Honey Springs' sheriff. With a grin, Mack held out his hand.

"Sheriff Weaver. Great to see you."

"You as well. I'd like for you to drop by the station some time on Monday. There's certain things I need to converse with you about before you head back to Houston."

Philip saw he didn't convey his sympathies. Presumably on the grounds that the sheriff's work would be much simpler now that Peter was dead. What's more, he realized quite well Philip didn't need them.

"I can do that. I'll be here in some measure through the week's end so I can take care of a few potential issues. I haven't concluded how I will manage the house and land yet."

"Indeed, take a few time and consider it. Make certain to make the wisest decision for you." Charlie arrived at up and applauded Philip on the shoulder and pressed. "Seeing you, Philip is great. You've found real success. Your mother would have been glad."

As Charlie left, Philip contemplated his mom. She had passed on when he was five, so his recollections of her were unclear. He recalled her snickering and grinning a great deal. What's more, she gave him heaps of embraces. Now and again, he could nearly smell her aroma. She passed on excessively youthful because of an alcoholic driver. Sort of unexpected that his dad went to liquor after her demise. The container turned into his closest companion. What's more, Philip came to be only an excruciating indication of the family they used to be.

Chapter 2

The smell of consuming bacon shocked Susan back to the present. Fortunately, it was somewhat extra fresh and not destroyed on the grounds that — indeed, it was bacon. She plated eggs, corn meal, and the extra firm bacon and set the plate in the pickup window. Her short-request cook, Cathy, was in the middle of stacking a plate of rolls in the broiler and the request was up so she dealt with it. She'd been dealing with things at the bistro since she was a high schooner. Her folks, Ransack and Ellen Fry, had opened the eatery, initially called the Honey Springs Coffee shop, when she was a child. She grew up there.

The cafe resembled the heartbeat of the town. Individuals came there, not exclusively to eat a decent, generous dinner, however to visit and giggle and at times cry. At the point when Susan's folks concluded they needed to purchase a RV and travel the nation over, Susan was more than arranged to jump in the driver's seat. She dominated and had a fabulous returning of sort and renamed the burger joint as Susan's Bistro. She actually served a similar essential menu, however presently offered a couple of solid decisions too. She was doing what she cherished and she was totally satisfied. Her occupation was testing and tomfoolery and she had loved ones who cherished her. What else might she at some point care about? What about a man who stays close by?

After Cathy got back to her station, Susan strolled to the front counter to keep an eye on her clients and was more than happy to see her companion Carly. They had been rigid companions since secondary school.

"Hello, young lady. I know you're en route to Little Shake to see Lucy. Make certain to give her an embrace for me, OK?"

"I will. Unfortunate thing. She's truly making some intense memories. That man she wedded is a flat out butt," Carly said, shaking her head.

Susan gave her companion an embrace and said, "Watch out. I'll converse with you when you get back. The morning meal swarm earlier today is greater than expected."

"Better believe it, I'm certain there's a major buzz about Peter Browne's passing and how Philip will manage the house and land."

Disregarding her clients briefly, Susan considered, "Indeed, I would envision he'd simply sell it. At the end of the day, he hasn't come back in seven years. Most likely has a spouse and children over in Houston. He has not an obvious explanation to return now."

Susan truly had no clue about what Philip had been doing during the time he'd been no more. She'd heard he was in Houston barely a year after he'd previously left. She'd never requested subtleties. She would have rather not known. Obviously what they'd had when they were more youthful made next to no difference to him, since he left without a farewell and never endeavored to reach her. Indeed, they'd been youthful. Be that as it may, she actually recalled how he'd affected her. How he'd said he adored her. He could have been the main man to mislead her. However, he unquestionably hadn't been the last.

The kitchen was being barraged by orders from hungry clients, so Hannah told Carly farewell and rushed to the back to help.

Monday Morning, Philip left the Honey Springs Bed and Breakfast stunned he'd had such a great amount for breakfast. Despite the fact that he just mentioned espresso from Mrs. Hodges, she concluded he wanted waffles, dribbling with margarine and genuine maple syrup, and a western omelet, loaded down with onions, peppers, and bacon. Mrs. Hodges probably been right since he figured out how to eat each and every nibble. He'd need to figure out an opportunity this week to go for a run, or he'd be not doing so well when he got back to Houston. At this moment, however, he'd forego driving his truck and simply stroll to the sheriff's office all things considered.

He had no clue about why Charlie needed to meet with him. While they hadn't remained nearby with one another since Philip had left town, Charlie had called Philip a few times each year to ask how he was doing. Philip expected the topic of Charlie's discussion earlier today would be in some way connected with Peter Browne's passing. It didn't exactly make any difference. Philip was grateful to have an impermanent interruption. He'd put off the gig of getting his dad's — his — house tidied up and prepared to sell. Peter had truly allowed the spot to go while he'd gradually drank himself to death. The house needed fixes and the yard was surprisingly more dreadful. The grass hadn't been cut in a long time, and the patio was covered with heaps of brew jars and bourbon bottles.

Essentially the state of the home destroyed no great recollections he'd had of it. Since he didn't have any.

He strolled past the recreation area toward the sheriff's office and halted when he saw the gazebo. The main kiss he'd imparted to Susan had been in that gazebo. He recalled that evening like it was yesterday. They had watched the town's fourth of July light show and afterward withdrew into the shadows of the little nook. As he pondered that first hint of their lips, he reviewed different firsts they'd shared too.

Unexpectedly, rather than seeing the gazebo, he saw Susan loosened up on a sweeping by the waterway, the evening glow radiating on her delightful bare body. Her arms raised to go after him as he gradually sank into — The recognizable tune of chapel chimes rang out, surprising him out of his dream. The chimes rung multiple times to report the hour. He started strolling at a lively speed now as he preferred not to be late.

He strolled in the entryway of the station to see Charlie at the back counter, pouring some espresso.

"Philip, return on," called the sheriff and promptly started pouring one more cup for Mack.

They strolled back to his office, and Charlie pushed the entryway shut.

He took a taste of his espresso, put down his cup and said, "I'm about to get to the point. I'm wanting to resign sooner rather than later. I believe that you should have my spot here as sheriff."

Philip stifled a little on the espresso he'd quite recently gulped.

"What? You must be joking."

"I'm intense. I need to resign. Got some grand babies I need to invest more energy with. I've followed your profession throughout the long term and I know you're really great person for the gig." He paused for a minute and took one more taste of his espresso.

"Look," Philip said as he reclined in his seat. "I'm complimented. Truly. However, when I wrap things up with the house and land, I'm returning to Houston. Furthermore, don't you have somebody here as of now who'd be intrigued?"

"I have two part time appointees. Nor is qualified or even somewhat intrigued." Charlie polished off the last piece of espresso in his cup. "Simply think about it, alright? No one can say for sure. You could alter your perspective."

Philip shook his head. "Not likely. However, I'll consider it." He stood up and held his hand out to the next man. "You know. I don't think I at any point truly said thanks to you for how you helped me such a long time back. Thus, much obliged."

Charlie shook Philip's hand and said, "Just made the right decision. You did all the difficult work. Inform me as to whether there's anything I can do to help this week. Simply recall. The work's yours assuming that you need it."

"Regardless of whether I were intrigued — which I'm not — wouldn't that need endorsement from the town board?" Mack didn't know why he was in any event, inquiring.

"That's right. However, I previously ran it past them. They concurred."

Philip checked out at Charlie with a statement of doubt and shock. "I — I don't actually have the foggiest idea what to think about that. At the end of the day, how might they consent to employ somebody for the gig of sheriff without meeting them or getting references or — "

"Simple. I suggested you. Also, when I recorded every one of the advancements and grants you'd got, indeed, they concurred with me."

Philip just shook his head and chuckled. "Unfathomable."

Charlie shrugged and said, "May not be the way they get things done in Houston, yet that is the way it works in Honey Springs. Consider it."

Philip indeed shook Charlie's hand. "I will. Yet, no commitments."

He left the station and into the cool November air. Damn, I didn't see that coming. Of the relative multitude of things Charlie might have conversed with him about, for all intents and purposes offering him the place of head of police absolutely wasn't one of them. Well, it's crazy to figure I would simply move back to Honey Springs and become sheriff. Isn't it?

"Thus, Have You Conversed with Philip since he's been visiting the area?" Carly Watkins requested in the wake of gulping her significant piece from pizza.

Each Monday night, the two companions met for pizza and a film. What's more, wine. For quite a long time, it had been their approach to remaining associated with one another. Sara Hart came when she was capable, which wasn't frequently since she was attempting to get past school. She took the base class load permitted with her awards and worked each accessible hour she had. Lucy Harris was hitched and living in Little Stone, so she hadn't partaken for some time now. However, that might be changing in the future due to her forthcoming separation.

"I addressed him after his father's administrations." Hannah topped off their wineglasses.

"Well?" Carly asked restlessly.

"Well what?" Susan asked while perusing her film assortment.

"What did you all discussion about? Did you ask him for what good reason he left you between a rock and a hard place a long time back? How's he going to manage the house and land? Could it be said that he is moving back? Could it be said that he is hitched? Have any children?" Carly ticked off her inquiries as though she were examining the adversary.

Susan murmured. "I let him know I was upset for his misfortune."

" Gosh?"

Susan badly creased her nose and said, "He could have expressed something about needing to get together and talk."

"I knew it! So when are you meeting him?" Carly asked enthusiastically.

"Um. I'm not. I let him know I didn't think it was smart." Susan took one more chomp of her pizza.

"Good gracious, Susan! Is there any valid reason why you

wouldn't have any desire to converse with him? Don't you need to understand what happened such a long time back? Could it be said that you are interested by any means?"

"Obviously, I'm somewhat inquisitive. Yet, what great could it do now? Nothing will change. So why dig all that up once more?" Susan shook her head and took a taste of wine.

"All in all, in the event that you don't mind somehow, why not converse with him? He clearly needs to tell you or he could not have possibly requested to get together." Carly squinted her eyes and checked Susan out. "Is there some other motivation behind why you would rather not converse with him?"

Susan murmured and afterward conceded, "I simply don't have any desire to work up any of my old sentiments about him, you know? Other than my father, the men who've been a major part of my life don't actually keep close by. I don't have to begin thinking 'consider the possibility that' about Mack. I have my eatery and I'm content."

A sprinkle of misery was in Carly's eyes when she said, "That's what I get. I truly do. Yet, perhaps assuming you went into it with simply the possibility of at last accepting reality for what it is, that would help."

"I'll consider it. Once more, he likely won't actually ask." Susan polished off her glass of wine and presented herself with another. "In this way, enlighten me concerning your date Saturday night."

Carly fanned her face and said, "Girl, on the off chance that I was keen on keeping a man around, he would've been in my main three!"

As Carly shook on about the occasions of her new date, Susan couldn't resist the opportunity to ponder the time she'd enjoyed with Philip in secondary school. She'd been so youthful and in adoration. She'd thought they'd be together until the end of time. What's more, she'd thought Philip had felt the same way. Clearly, he hadn't, since he'd left without a farewell and no contact from that point forward. She'd been crushed. With the assistance of her loved ones, she'd moved past him. Also, continuously, she'd gone from miserable to furious. Sooner or later, the outrage also had passed and she acknowledged the way that he simply hadn't cherished her the manner in which she'd adored him.

She'd had a few long haul connections from that point forward. Yet, they at last left her, as well. Their reasons differed from finding a new line of work out of state and not needing a remote relationship to simply dropping out of adoration. She wouldn't agree that she had abandoned love. She simply wasn't effectively looking for it. On the off chance that it ended up going along, fine. If not, she was good with that also. Since that was the situation, is there any good reason why she shouldn't meet with Philip? Perhaps it would serve to at long last get an opportunity to let him know exactly how he'd treated her by leaving without a word. The more she mulled over everything, the more she preferred the thought. She would allow him to have it. And afterward it would be finished. At long last.

Three

Chapter 3

Philip enjoyed some time off from getting garbage in the yard of his young life home. He'd been busy since early morning and it didn't seem as though he'd made a mark yet. It was basically impossible that he would have been ready to do this whole work himself. He'd just requested seven days off from work. Since he'd had the option to make all the memorial service game plans by telephone, so there truly wasn't a thing he expected to do once he reached town Friday night. He'd assumed he'd have everything dealt with at the property by this end of the week, yet that was before he'd seen exactly the way in which terrible things had gotten. Recruiting a cleanup group was his main genuine decision. No chance would he sort out for a Realtor to come take a gander at the spot while it was not doing so well.

A brief glance at his watch let him know it was noon. He was amazed to acknowledge he was ravenous. At the point when he'd left the B&B today, he'd sworn he'd at no point ever eat in the future. Mrs. Hodges had served a flavorful breakfast dish with colossal hand crafted rolls loaded up with spread and blackberry jam. He'd eaten more than he ought to have, yet he was unable to stop himself. With how much work he confronted tidying this spot up, it was no issue working off those additional calories.

Since he was a masochist, he headed his truck toward Susan's Bistro. She'd passed him over when he told her he needed to talk, yet he trusted she'd rethink. For a really long time, he'd had the option to push everything about Susan and Honey Springs from his brain. He'd zeroed in on his vocation, and his commitment had paid off when he'd been elevated to analyst.

Be that as it may, presently, since he'd come back in Honey Springs, the sum of everything on his mind was Susan. It was presumably only his sensations of responsibility and regret, despite the fact that he'd let himself know again and again that he had nothing to feel remorseful for. He'd done how he needed to save his life. After that night…his the previous evening in Honey Springs…there was no chance he might have remained. His main decision was to leave and cut attaches with everybody. Indeed, nearly everybody.

So presently, he got an opportunity to make sense of. To confess all with the one individual he never suspected he'd hurt. Assuming she would simply listen to him. He pulled up to the cafe and strolled inside, searching for a vacant table. He seen one toward the back and advanced there. He'd seen Susan immediately. She was conversing with a couple situated on the opposite side of the lounge area while she topped off their glasses with sweet tea. She chuckled at something the lady said and Philip's heart skirted a thump.

God, he'd missed her. He hadn't understood exactly how much until this exact second. He'd constantly pushed those considerations from his psyche. He'd have always been unable to work in the event that he'd permitted himself to ponder Hannah to an extreme. For his own self-protection, he'd needed to compel those sentiments back. Yet, presently? When she was directly before him? He proved unable. Crap. He shouldn't have come here. He'd persuaded himself he simply needed to talk. Yet, presently, he needed more. He needed to hold her. Contact her. Kiss her.

As the couple from the table advanced out, he saw Susan check the space to check whether some other clients required consideration. Her eyes associated with his and she promptly stilled. He looked as she appeared to gather herself and traveled his direction, halting to get a menu en route to his table.

Susan grinned brilliantly as she put the menu on his table.

"You most likely believe a couple of moments should investigate the menu. What could I at any point inspire you to drink?" She held her eyes down on the request cushion she removed from her cover.

"Sweet tea, please. Susan — "

"The exceptional today is vegetable soup with a dish hamburger sandwich on French bread. Yet again I'll be right back with your tea, she had an unusually large grin all over as she dismissed and strolled.

Philip attempted to focus on the menu, yet he continually thought of himself as looking through her out. God, she was lovely. No big surprise he'd fallen hard for her in secondary school. During that time, she was the main splendid spot in his miserable, sad life. It almost killed him to leave her. Be that as it may, it would have in a real sense killed him in the event that he'd remained.

He watched her methodology with his beverage, her grin currently missing. She set the glass on the table, and on second thought of leaving or requesting to take his request, she plunked down in the seat opposite him, fastened her hands together and laid them on the table. He saw that they were shudder marginally.

She took a full breath in through her nose and said, "If your proposal to talk is still on the table, I might want to do that."

He read up her face briefly and gestured. "Indeed, I'd like that definitely. Where and when might you want to meet?"

"Could tomorrow night around six thirty? My place? I live in a similar house as…before." She jotted down her location on her request cushion and removed the page to provide for him. "The exceptional tomorrow is lasagna. I can bring some home and we can eat first assuming you like."

He wasn't amazed at her liberality. "I'd like that. Much thanks to you."

She grinned pleasantly, and Philip's mouth went totally dry. His heart hurt for what might have and ought to have been between them.

"Thus, did you conclude what you might want to eat?" Susan asked, her pen ready to record his request, as the tip of her tongue momentarily contacted her upper lip.

Philip's eyes were right away attracted to her mouth. Child, I know precisely very thing I might want to eat. Also, it ain't on the menu. Susan's grin wavered a little and for a heart-halting second, Philip stressed he'd said those words without holding back. He understood he was gazing and intellectually gave himself a shake. In the wake of making a sound as if to speak, he took a speedy taste of his tea and said, "The extraordinary sounds perfect. Much obliged."

His food was conveyed to him a brief time later and he dove in. The soup was delectable with large lumps of vegetables. The sandwich was overstuffed with broil hamburger and accompanied additional sauce and heaps of napkins. As he ate, he got looks at Susan and began to consider how he planned to endure when it was only both of them in her home. Then, at that point, he recollected everything he expected to say to her, and his energy diminished. He didn't know what he expected to acquire by making sense of what happened such a long time prior. He realized they didn't have a future together. Perhaps it would be sufficient on the off chance that she simply didn't detest him any longer.

For the third time in under ten minutes, Susan glanced through the window to check whether Philip had shown up yet. Take a few to get back some composure, young lady. Dislike he's coming over for a date. At the point when he arrives, we'll eat and afterward I'll allow him to have some appropriately harsh criticism. Relentless pacing was supplanted with getting all worked up about the garlic bread in the stove until it was flawlessly seared. A lucky call from her mom forestalled a third round of salad preparing. Her mom called to tell her they'd be getting back home for Thanksgiving in half a month. They were partaking in their movements along the East Coast yet were restless to get back for a little while. Her mom cheerfully discussed every one of the spots they'd been as of late and their arrangements for the following week or so until the time had come to go to Honey Springs. Susan couldn't hold back to see them and quickly started arranging the menu for their Thanksgiving supper. Similarly as she detached the call, she heard a thump on the entryway.

She paused for a minute to inhale and afterward serenely strolled to the front entryway, taking as much time as is needed. Permitting him to see she was apprehensive about his visit just wouldn't do. At the point when she opened the entryway, she saw him investigating at the patio swing to one side. She contemplated whether he was recollecting the hours they spent there, talking, checking out at the stars and sneaking kisses. He went then to take a gander at her and grinned. She was almost certain he'd been recalling exactly the same thing.

His eyes met hers and he said, "Man, it doesn't appear as though anything's changed here by any means."

She grinned firmly and said, "Nothing stays the equivalent until the end of time. Enter. I trust you're eager. I brought a lot of lasagna home from the bistro."

As he strolled in, he considered the open front room. Absolutely not a chance he could not say anything had changed now, thought Susan. She was glad for the manner in which the room looked and felt, with light dim walls and a dim, nearly naval force emphasize wall on the opposite side of the room. She had picked a major, comfortable love seat in a cereal tone, and she'd nicely organized dazzling orange and naval force pads all through. There were two side seats canvassed in a naval force and white mathematical example. Those tones continued into the kitchen region, with a similar dull dark/blue variety on the cupboards and white rock ledges. The general look was basic and delightful.

Philip gestured in appreciation as his eyes took in everything about. "Mrs. Hodges from the B&B said your folks invest their energy voyaging now?"

Susan drove Philip to the kitchen and motioned for him to sit down at the bar. "Could you like something to drink? I have lager, wine, sweet tea…"

"Sweet tea, please."

While Susan filled a glass with tea, she said, "OK, they said following quite a while of being secured to the cafe, they needed to spread their wings. Despite the fact that, rather than flying, they're driving. They purchased a RV and simply go any place they need. They love it."

"What might be said about you?" Philip requested in the wake of taking a taste from his beverage. "Now that you're running the cafe, do you feel the same way? Secured?"

Susan shrugged as she got her own glass of tea. "I don't have any idea. I have to take a hard pass. Mother and Father generally preferred to deal with most things all alone. I've been sufficiently fortunate to discover a few great, reliable individuals to work with. I can leave for a couple of days and feel sure that all that will be dealt with. I have some secondary school kids who come in to help, particularly over the summers. They like the additional cash and I like the additional adaptability in my timetable. I have a concurrence with the secondary school to give preparing on independent work, so they can get some genuine work insight along with credits toward graduation. It's been an encounter working with a great deal of similar educators we had while we were in school. Many of them are as yet pushing ahead."

Philip's eyebrows raised. "Indeed, even Mr. Gun?"

Susan had quite recently taken a taste of her tea. She slapped her hand over her mouth and rushed to swallow so she wouldn't let it out. "Gracious amazing. I haven't contemplated Mr. Gun for a long time!" Susan tapped her chest with her hand.

Philip smiled and inquired, "Do you recollect that time he

heated up a container of soup on the Bunsen burner in science class and it bubbled over? I can in any case recollect that smell!"

Snickering, Susan said, "And afterward, when he attempted to snatch the can off the burner, he dropped it since it was so hot. Soup went all over the place, the burner spilled and some paper towels burst into flames."

Philip snickered. "And afterward Sam Rolling got the fire roused and showered the whole table and the majority of the floor." Philip continued to copy Sam employing the fire quencher with extraordinary energy.

The mix of the recollections, alongside Philip's re-sanctioning of Sam with the fire roused, was simply too amusing Susan giggled until she had tears in her eyes and her stomach hurt. She cleaned her eyes with her hands and when she looked into, Philip was taking a gander at her and grinning, his eyes warm and cheerful. Also, by and by, she was hit with the acknowledgment of what she might have had. What they might have had. Together. In the event that he hadn't left without a word.

Philip saw the adjustment of her appearance and sobered. Susan contemplated whether he'd arrive at a similar understanding too.

At the point when it looked like Philip planned to say something different, Susan shouted out all things being equal. "For what reason don't we feel free to eat. We can talk later."

Mack's eyes scanned her face briefly and afterward he gestured and said, "I'd like that."

Despite his fear about let Susan know what happened such an extremely long time back, Philip acknowledged he was really living it up. Susan was similarly as thoughtful, wonderful and kind as she'd been the point at which they were more youthful. God, it appeared to be a lifetime prior. He'd been so credulous and inept. In the event that you simply don't discuss what's happening at home, it's not genuine. Isn't that so? All in all, how'd that turn out for you? He could never have been all the more off-base.

The environment changed radically when they started to eat. They went from snickering and thinking back about the past to awkward casual discussion. He was torn. A piece of him needed to simply get everything out in the open and done so he could leave, and one more piece of him simply needed to remain close to her however long he could.

The lasagna was heavenly. Susan was clearly quite a cook. Yet, as he pondered everything that he expected to say to her, it went to sawdust in his mouth. He figured out how to get done with eating what was on his plate, yet when he looked over at Hannah's, she'd scarcely eaten anything.

With a surrendered look all over, Susan stood up and said, "For what reason don't we go into the front room so we can…talk. I have a few things I want to share with you. Things I've needed — required — to tell you for quite a while."

Philip stood and the two of them carried their plates to the sink and afterward strolled into the lounge. Philip sat in one of the side seats while Susan sank down on the sofa. For some time, she didn't express anything while she followed a nonexistent example on her pants. Philip watched her intently and intellectually prepared himself for what he knew was to come.

Susan turned upward out of nowhere, gulped hard and inquired, "Do you know how you treated me when you just left without a word? Without a clarification? Without a farewell?" Her lower lip shuddered somewhat and she seemed to battle to keep up with control of her feelings. She peered down again briefly as though she were gathering her boldness. At long last, she took a gander at him and said, "I cherished you, Philip. It might have been a youthful, young love, yet it was genuine and valid. What's more, I thought — " Her voice broke marginally. "I thought you adored me, as well. You let me know you did."

Fuck. Philip wouldn't give himself an out by shutting his eyes or turning away. She had the right to have her pound of tissue and she'd held up quite a while to get it. In this way, he'd simply stay here and take it. He owed her that much.

She had all the earmarks of being drawing up her inward strength as she fixed her shoulders and shifted her jaw somewhat higher. "Yet, I suppose I'm not the principal young lady to be taken care of a line just so a person could get in her jeans." The skeptical look all over was just…wrong. His Susan had consistently checked out at the brilliant side of things. In the event that there was a silver lining, she'd track down it.

While he'd let himself know he'd allow her to talk and express her opinion, he just couldn't allow her last assertion to remain without a reaction. "I never took care of you a line. All that I shared with you in those days was valid. I cherished you. Also, it almost annihilated me when I needed to leave."

"Why? For what reason did you leave without a word? For what reason did you leave by any stretch of the imagination? I simply don't have the foggiest idea. You just vanished suddenly."

It was right here. The second he'd been fearing. He planned to recount his story, ask for her pardoning and then…what? Continue on?

Philip stood and paced the length of the room. When he pivoted, he said, "You know that my mother kicked the bucket when I was five, right?"

Susan gestured. Her eyes never left Philip's face.

"Indeed, after she kicked the bucket, Peter basically self-destructed. He concluded he favored the organization of a bourbon container to his child." He shrugged. "From the get go, he'd simply drink a little at night after supper. In the long run, bourbon turned into his supper. I ate a ton of sandwiches and cold oat growing up. As the years went on, Peter drank to an ever increasing extent. Ultimately, he just drank constantly."

Philip shook his head as the recollections surfaced. "For quite a while, he just disregarded me. He didn't get mean until I was somewhat more seasoned and became keen on young ladies.

Perhaps he didn't maintain that I should have what he could never have." He shook his head. "Or on the other hand perhaps he was only an alcoholic, disdainful bastard. At last, he became physical. I attempted to avoid his direction admirably well, however I needed to ultimately return home. I didn't have elsewhere to go."

Susan made some noise. "You might have let somebody know occurring. They would have helped you."

Philip grinned unfortunately at that. "He couldn't ever have let me go elsewhere. I would have needed to leave town totally." He shook his head and laughed with next to no genuine humor. "Needed to do that at any rate eventually."

Philip strolled back over to his seat and plunked down. "Generally, he was mindful so as to not make any apparent imprints. Thus, remaining beneath the radar was quite simple."

The expression all over almost destroyed him.

"For what reason didn't you at any point let me know what was happening? You might have let me know anything. For what reason didn't you trust me?"

He could hear the hurt and disarray in her voice, and the last thing he needed was to make her think that any of this was her issue.

He rose from his seat and afterward plunked down close to her on the lounge chair. Since he just couldn't help himself, he tenderly measured her face in his grasp, his thumb moving delicately over her cheek and sanctuary.

"I never believed any of that grotesqueness should contact you. Also, all things considered, I was youthful. Also, arrogant. Also, I figured I could deal with everything all alone. I didn't need anybody feeling frustrated about me. Plus, I had everything arranged out. We'd complete school. Then I'd find a new line of work, wed you, and we'd live joyfully ever later." He dropped his hand, peered down and shut his eyes briefly to gather his considerations. Since the most awful piece of his story was on the way.

"So what ended up evolving that?" asked Susan.

Philip cleaned his undoubtedly his face and moaned. Should get it over with.

"Do you recall that the previous evening we were together?"

Susan gestured and said, "obviously. We had gone to the football match-up at the secondary school." Her face turned somewhat pink when she added, "And we went to the riverbank and… made love."

He gestured, recollecting their last time together also. It had played to him over and over throughout the long term.

"All things considered, Peter probably seen us when we got once again into town. He was heading back home from the Hey Ball Bar. He was holding up from me when I returned home. He began in on me when I strolled in the entryway. Letting me know he'd seen us and that in the event that he didn't have anybody, then, at that point, I could never have anybody. I attempted to overlook him since he was simply in another tipsy fury." Philip automatically grasped and clenched his clench hands. "In any case, when he began saying that I was only a kid, and that perhaps you should have been with a genuine man…" He stopped briefly and afterward said, "That is when things gained out of influence. He recently continued saying these revolting and horrendous things about how he could treat you, and afterward he took a swing at me. And…I lost it. I began hitting him and, obviously, he was totally squandered. He fell and I bounced on top of him and recently continued to hit him." Philip gulped the bile in his throat and proceeded. "I recently continued to hit him until Sheriff Weaver removed me from him. In the event that he wasn't there…I think…I figure I would have killed him."

After this admission, there was finished quiet. He'd never said those words without holding back. He had thoroughly considered them a lot of times the years. However, some way or another, saying it just made it that much more…horrific. He would have rather not seen the appearance of nausea he knew would be in Hannah's eyes.

"Sheriff Weaver realized I wouldn't have the option to remain there after what had occurred. He knew a resigned Houston PD chief. He called him and inquired as to whether I could remain with him for some time. Essentially until I could get a new line of work and stand up. Hank and Cart Thatcher saved my life. I was a finished fucking wreck when I arrived promptly the following morning. With help from the Thatchers, I had the option to get my secondary school equivalency declaration and Hank assisted me with continuing ahead with the Houston PD as a representative from the get go since I was just eighteen. In a hurry, I applied for freshman school. Furthermore, I've been there from that point onward."

He stopped briefly to accumulate his considerations. Susan hadn't provided him with any signs of how she had an outlook on what he'd recently uncovered to her. In any case, he realize that her reaction to what he needed to say next would decide his likely arrangements.

"Please accept my apologies I put you through all that. My main reason is that I was a youngster attempting to take care of business. Also, in the event that I was bound to turn into my dad, I didn't believe you should see that. Then, at that point, after such a lot of time passed by, I figured you'd previously continued on and it was an exercise in futility to remember all that occurred. At the point when I saw you at the burial service, I wanted to let you know all that had occurred and request your pardoning."

He hung tight for her reaction, unwittingly pausing his breathing. The following words out of her mouth destroyed him.

Four

Chapter 4

"Are you cracking difficult, Philip Brownsville?Susan could scarcely hold back her indignation.

"Susan — "

Susan stood up, hands on her hips and nearly vibrating with rage. "No! You've expressed your opinion. Presently I will have mine. I couldn't actually accept you recently said that. Why for heaven's sake could you at any point feel that you were bound to turn into your dad? That is the outright most ridiculous thing I've heard. You were never similar to your dad. You were caring and thoughtful. Delicate. Fun. Cherishing. You generally caused me to feel exceptional. I won't ever accept there's even a chance you could become like him."

When she got done with talking, she was at this point not

furious. She felt emptied and only miserable as she sank down in her seat. "I am so sorry you went through all that. I comprehend the reason why you didn't and couldn't express anything in those days. Furthermore, I'm happy you let me know now. You were valuable to me and I've loathed detesting you."

Susan felt help as she let go of that weight. While it hadn't been anything she'd fixated on, basically not after the main year of Philip's vanishing, it had kept on annoying at the rear of her psyche. Also, at times, the very easiest thing would set off her, and the recollections would come streaming back.

By the alleviated look all over, she envisioned he felt the same way. Albeit, presently, she wasn't exactly certain where they should go from here. Susan made a sound as if to speak and said, "Thus, um, I surmise this implies we can be companions now."

"I'd like that. Without question," Philip said.

With a gesture, Susan inquired, "How long would you say you are wanting to remain around?"

Philip scowled and said, "Initially, I thought I'd get the house fixed up and afterward put it available. Be that as it may, I didn't understand exactly the way in which awful things had arrived. I've pondered mentioning some downtime so I can finish all that without feeling surged. I have no less than about a month set aside that I could utilize."

Susan gestured and attempted to consider the most effective way to pose the inquiry she'd been passing on to inquire. She peered down to pick a fanciful piece of build up from her pants and inquired, "All in all, assuming you will remain that long, will your sweetheart show up also? Or then again your better half?"

Shaking his head, Philip answered, "All things considered, since I don't have a sweetheart or spouse, I'll be solo."

His response just raised around 1,000,000 different inquiries. Is it true or not that he was between sweethearts? Or on the other hand more awful, would he say he in the middle between spouses? Did he have a spouse previously? For what reason do you try and need to be aware, Hannah?

"And you? Do you have a sweetheart or spouse concealing in the room?" Philip asked in a kidding yet not-kidding way.

"No, I'm apprehensive not," Susan replied with a murmur.

Philip took a gander at Susan, his eyes clearing over her face and perhaps, quite possibly they waited all the rage for somewhat excessively lengthy. "Are the men in this town blind?"

Susan grinned tragically. "Let's just get real for a moment, they unquestionably approve of their legs and feet."

Confounded, Philip inquired, "Your meaning could be a little more obvious."

With a shrug, she said, "They generally leave."

There was a glimmer of culpability in Philip's eyes, and Susan truly didn't have any desire to harp on her absence of long haul connections, so she immediately switched up the conversation. "In this way, educate me regarding your work in Houston. You said you'd as of late gotten advanced? That is energizing."

Fortunately, Philip took the lure and permitted the difference in subject. They discussed his work and her life at the bistro until late at night.

At the point when Philip's telephone hummed with an approaching message, he looked down at it. "Amazing, I didn't understand how late it was. I envision you must be at the bistro promptly in the first part of the day. I didn't intend to remain so lengthy. I'll get rolling so you can get to bed."

The two of them stood and said, "I truly appreciated finding you. I forgot about the time, as well."

"Much obliged to you. For everything." Philip delayed the slightest bit and inquired, "Could I at any point give you an embrace?"

Susan grinned and said, "I'd like that."

She quickly felt areas of strength for him fold over her, and he held her tight for a significant length of time. His fingers on her midsection moved to and fro, somewhat, the lightest of strokes. She had brought her arms moving around his neck and held him near her too. She needed to transform her face into his neck and inhale him in. The mix of cleanser and man was inebriating. What's more, for reasons unknown, that made her need to cry. Since as it were, he was the standard, worn out Philip. However at that point once more, he was additionally similar to an outsider.

At long last, his arms released their hang on her and they drew separated, however not totally. They kept on remaining there as though they were each reluctant to break contact by and large. Philip's eyes frequently wandered to Susan's mouth and briefly, she thought he planned to kiss her. However at that point, she watched him swallow hard and afterward leisurely move back totally.

"Could you go out to supper with me this end of the week? I'd truly prefer to see you again before I pass on to return home," Philip inquired.

Her most memorable intuition was to say no, however she was unable to stand up to. The same old thing there, Susan. You were unable to oppose him in secondary school all things considered.

Gesturing, she grinned and said, "I'd like that."

"Amazing. I'll get you Saturday night? Around six?"

"That sounds perfect. I'll see you then," Susan said, previously anticipating their...what? Date? Probably not. Goodbye meeting with a companion. Some way or another, that didn't cause her to feel improved.

Back in his room at the Honey Springs B&B, Philip continued to replay the night with Hannah again and again. It was such a help to realize she comprehended the motivations behind why he needed to leave, and in particular, she'd excused him. Yet, this liberating sensation prompted other confounding sentiments. What was next for them? Could they turn out to be significant distance companions and send messages, talk periodically, and trade Christmas cards? Perhaps he'd persuaded himself before that could be sufficient, yet presently? After he'd embraced her once more? He wasn't entirely certain.

He'd nearly kissed her. And afterward he'd recalled that he wasn't remaining in Honey Springs, and he didn't do connections. What's more, Susan was not the indulgence type. She was the sort of lady you remained with. The sort of lady you could construct a daily existence and family with. Furthermore, that wasn't what was going on with he.

Their supper on Saturday night would be absolutely dispassionate. He would do nothing to lead her on or play with her feelings. He wouldn't hurt her once more.

Philip switched off the television, not that he'd gave any consideration to anything playing, and had quite recently reached to turn off the bedside light when his telephone rang. A fast look at the guest ID let him know it was his accomplice, Ryan. "Hello, man. What's happening?" Philip said.

"Getting fucking burnt out on pursuing the trouble makers here without help from anyone else," Ryan grumbled.

"I'm making a beeline for Houston on Sunday. I'll be back to business as usual on Monday. There will constantly be all the more trouble makers. Relax," Mack expressed, resting back up against the headboard.

"Things have been peaceful on the Rostropovich case. Makes me wonder when the crap will raise a ruckus around town," Ryan said.

"Fuck," said Philip. "It's terrible enough that the South American medication cartels have started to appreciate Houston. However, presently we have the Russians attempting to get a traction and irritating the Escaroles. I question everybody will hide out a lot of longer. They're most likely all making another arrangement on how they can kill each other quicker."

"Ain't that the buckskin truth," Ryan said. "Is it true or not that you were ready to manage everything around there?"

Philip extinguished a breath. "No, man. The whole house and property is pretty screwed up. I will finish however much I can this week, yet I'm thinking I'll have to take a portion of my get-away to complete everything. It's not worth a lot now on the off chance that I choose to sell."

"If? You're pondering keeping the spot? Why?" Ryan inquired.

Until that second, Philip hadn't understood he was thinking about that. "I don't have the foggiest idea. Simply keeping every one of my choices open."

"That is cool. I'll let you go and I'll see you on Monday, man," Ryan said as he detached.

Why in the world could I try and think about keeping the house? Right away, Susan's grinning face showed up in his mind. And afterward the memory of holding Peter down and hitting him. Again and again. What's more, finished. Shaking his head and sickened with himself for contemplating the chance of remaining in Honey Springs, he turned off the light and attempted to get some rest.

The remainder of the week passed rapidly for Susan. To the surprise of no one, the bistro had a constant flow of clients for both breakfast and lunch. The cafe had turned into the put to get and get together on the most recent news. As she got out and about to each table all through the lounge area, she heard scraps of discussions. "Peter sure let the property go. His kid has a ton of work to do there…I can't help thinking about how he will manage the spot once he sorts it out up…I trust he doesn't offer the spot to a developer…Maybe he'll choose to remain once he gets everything back in shape…From what I hear, he's some hotshot Houston investigator. There's no great explanation for him to come back…Oh. My. God. Peter Brownsville is the most blazing thing to go to this town in a really long time!"

Susan unquestionably couldn't contend with that last assertion. Peter had forever been gorgeous. In any case, presently? He resembled sex on a stick. Susan shook her head and snickered to herself. Presently you sound very much like Carly.

A few times this week, she'd saw individuals would turn away out of nowhere when she discovered them watching her. She guessed they were interested about her opinion on Philip being back in the area after so much time. A couple of them were even sufficiently strong to ask inside and out on the off chance that she knew for what valid reason Philip had left so out of nowhere. She kept her reactions unclear and would just agree that that she guessed he had his reasons. All things considered, it wasn't her story to tell.

Saturday morning, Carly came by Susan's home to get her. They'd made arrangements weeks prior to go out to shop in Rock port. Rock port was the following town over and had a decent shopping center and choice of shops. When Carly turned onto the interstate, the inquiries started. "Anyway, how was your date an evening or two ago with Philip? Did you all get an opportunity to talk? Did you figure out why he left without a word to anybody?"

"Decent, yes and yes." Hannah giggled.

"Come on, young lady. You know the drill. Spill it."

Susan proceeded to depict the night, including the conditions that let up to Philip leaving town such a long time back.

When Carly maneuvered into the shopping center parking area, Susan was making sense of about individuals who took Philip in when he showed up in Houston.

Carly was very nearly tears when she put the vehicle in

leave. Squinting quickly, she went to Susan and murmured, "Unfortunate Philip. I never thought he was being manhandled. Nobody did indeed. He shouldn't have needed to go through that by itself." Carly sniffed a couple of times and afterward said, "Indeed, basically you understand what happened now, and you don't need to ponder any longer."

Gesturing in arrangement, Susan said, "Despite the fact that it's not something I've contemplated continually these most recent couple of years, there was consistently this little pestering voice in my sub-conscience. Contemplating whether I'd accomplished something wrong, or on the other hand on the off chance that he'd quite recently utilized me until he chose to leave."

"All in all, what's the arrangement proceeding? Are you all going to keep in contact?" Carly reapplied her lipstick while searching in the visor reflect.

"I think we'd both like that. What's more, we have plans to go out to supper this evening. Sort of a goodbye visit before he passes on to return to Houston."

Carly threw her lipstick in her handbag and said, "That is so great! After seven years and you're having one more date with your secondary school crush."

"It's anything but a date. It's a we-are-about to visit-again-before-he-leaves-town sort of thing. Truly. It's anything but a date." Susan didn't know who she was attempting to persuade more...herself or Carly.

Not getting it, Carly said, "Indeed, I think you want something fantastic to wear on your not-date."

Susan grinned. "Presently you're talking.'"

As it would turn out, Susan found the ideal dress in the main store they visited. Profound burgundy in variety, the dress had a scooped neck area and charming erupted skirt. The scalloped stitch highlighted a sensitive laser-cut plan. It was pretty and coquettish without being excessively dressy or excessively easygoing. Susan fell head over heels for it and bought it right away. Carly concurred that it was the dress.

"You know," Carly said as they left the store, "I feel that is only the dress that could make Mack mull over returning to Houston."

Susan chuckled at the silly face Carly made, joined by overstated eyebrow raising. "Ha! He'd most likely need somewhat more than that to move to Honey Springs. Like perhaps a task?"

Carly took a gander at her companion and said truly, "No one can say for sure. Perhaps this should be your time, you know? Like this is all incident now on purpose."

"That is a decent thought, honey. However, I'm not going to let my imagination run wild for any such thing. I'm about to partake in my not-date this evening and reconnect with a past love interest."

They spent the remainder of the early daytime strolling, chasing after deals and whatever was simply too charming to even consider missing, and afterward had lunch at another Greek eatery they had both been needing to attempt.

During their tasty lunch of stuffed grape leaves and spanking, Carly enlightened Susan regarding her new encounter with Lucy.

"I'm truly stressed over Lucy Loo. She's recently crushed. Furthermore, confounded. Furthermore, indeed, lost," Carly said.

"I know. I feel so defenseless." Susan wounded furiously at her plate and said, "That man is such a jerk. I surmise he believes that since he has huge load of cash, he can deal with individuals like soil. She should be finished with him and return home so we can ensure she realizes who cherishes her."

"I concur with you there. Yet, I don't think she has any sort of plan for what to do straightaway," said Carly.

"She ought to make him pay in the separation. Swindle him. Really awful she's not someone like that," expressed Susan with a disturbed look all over.

"I think the main thing she's centered around right presently is simply moving away from him," Carly said as she shook her head tragically. "She was so down on herself while I was there. She believes she's a disappointment and she's humiliated about being utilized. It will require her a long investment to move past this."

"Fortunately, she has us," Susan said happily.

With reestablished energy from lunch, they left the shopping center and spent an unfathomable length of time in The Following Part book shop. Carly perused new youngsters' books while Susan inclined toward the food and recipes area. Their next stop was a tremendous specialty and side interest store, where they took a gander at all that from occasion designs to home stylistic layout. They weren't searching for anything specifically on the grounds that that was the most ideal sort of shopping.

At the point when their feet throbbed from strolling and their appearances hurt from grinning, the time had come to return home. At the point when Carly dropped her companion off at her home, she gave her a major embrace and, with a misrepresented wink, advised her to live it up on her not-date.

Five

Chapter 5

Subsequent to working at the house the entire day, Philip was unable to see any genuine improvement. The more he did, the more he found he expected to do. The greater part of the furniture was broken and dirty. There was junk in each room, with a variety of brew jars and bourbon bottles in the lounge and room. Everything went in the dumpster. Miserable that after such countless years, there was nothing valuable.

At three o'clock, he'd had enough and tapped out. He would have rather not been hurried to prepare for his date with Susan this evening. No. Not his date. His…evening out. Call it what you need, Philip. On the off chance that it seems to be a duck and quacks like a duck…

Coming back to the B&B, he halted to get gas at Rollins's Car and saw Sam Moving in one of the maintenance straights. Since he hadn't had a very remarkable opportunity to converse with Sam this week, he needed to basically express welcome before he went to Houston. Sam had his head in the engine of a 1964 Passage Horse that seemed as though it just fell off the display area floor.

At the point when Philip drew nearer, he called out to out Sam. Sam looked into, snatched a cloth and cleaned his hands prior to holding one out to Philip.

"Hello, man, I'm happy you come by. Been importance to call you to check whether you needed to go get a lager or something while you're still around."

Shaking his head with lament, Philip answered, "I'm passing on to make a beeline for Houston tomorrow, however I'm wanting to get some margin to wrap up the house. Thus, I'll find you when I get back in possibly 14 days."

"That is cool. I'm just about completed here. We could get together sometime in the evening."

"Apologies, man. That is out as well. I'm taking Susan out to supper this evening," Philip said, shaking his head.

Sam gave Philip a sideways look and inquired, "All in all, you all have gotten an opportunity to resolve things?"

Philip gestured. "After the administrations, I focused on conversing with Susan. We got an opportunity to talk and we're great at this point."

Sam scowled. "Very much like that?"

"I made sense of what occurred previously and apologized for harming her. She acknowledged my conciliatory sentiment, and we've consented to put that behind us so we can be companions. So this evening, I'm taking her to supper."

"That is great to hear, man. I'm happy you all got that settled. It's been quite a while." Sam looked really satisfied.

"No doubt, it felt far better to make sense of all that occurred in those days. Also, next time I'm visiting the area, I'll make sense of what befell you too." Philip didn't feel a similar degree of fear as before when he contemplated recounting his story to another person. As far as he could tell, in the event that Susan could comprehend and pardon him, why couldn't every other person?"

Sam shrugged. "I trust you had your reasons. If you have any desire to discuss it, fine. On the off chance that not, indeed, that is fine, as well."

"Much obliged, Sam. That's what I value." Philip thought back over at the Bronco and inquired, "Anyway, what's going on with the vehicle? Is it true that she is yours?"

Sam snickered and said, "I wish! It has a place with a gatherer in Little Stone. I might want to get more associated with reclamation, so perhaps this will be my pass to the game. This is what she resembled when I got her." Sam held up his telephone and looked at the photos.

"That is astounding, man. With an enchanted touch like that, your name ought to be Midas," Mack expressed, dazzled with the change.

Sam's eyebrows raised and he looked smart. "That's what I like. You may be on to something."

"Happy I could assist, man," said Mack. "I will run so I can get tidied up. I'll call you whenever I'm visiting the area."

A brief time later, Philip maneuvered into Susan's carport however faltered prior to getting out. His heart was beating ceaselessly in his chest and his palms were sweat-soaked. What in the world? He hadn't had an apprehensive outlook on a date since he was a first year recruit in secondary school. In any case, it was anything but a date. Only supper with a companion. That was all. That's it. So get a fucking hold, man.

Subsequent to sliding his undoubtedly his thighs to dry them, he took a full breath and escaped the vehicle. As he lifted his hand to thump on Susan's entryway, it abruptly opened and he nearly gulped his tongue. She. Was. Beautiful. What's more, on prompt, his heart beat against his chest and he misplaced all thought process.

"Goodness," said Susan, her hand on her chest. "I didn't anticipate that you should be there in a jiffy. I saw you drive up, yet when you didn't escape your vehicle, I thought something was off-base."

The main thing wrong is that I'm a fucking bonehead. "Sorry. I had a call." Method for going, Mack.

Susan grinned pleasantly and said, "Alright. Is it true or not that you are prepared to leave or would you like to come inside briefly?"

Assuming you go into her home at the present time, you could not at any point leave. "Could we simply feel free to go to the eatery? Let's be real, I could eat a pony." Philip intellectually slapped himself on the rear of his head. Smooth, Philip. Genuine smooth.

Susan snickered and said, "Gotcha. Allow me just to get my handbag."

It was a short drive to the eatery and fortunately, Hannah's prattle about her day shopping with Carly didn't need profound, significant discussion on his part. After his "eat a pony" proclamation prior, he believed it best to say as little as could really be expected.

The Italian cafe, Bella Mia, was little and close. As Mack sat opposite Hannah, the light from the flashing candle on the table moving across her face, he understood he was messing with himself. He would have rather not simply been companions. He needed a lot more. He had zero power over the occasions of the past. Be that as it may, he wasn't a kid any more. He was a man. What's more, he'd be condemned on the off chance that he planned to let Hannah go once more. He'd need to persuade her to allow him another opportunity. She'd gone gaga for him previously. Once more, perhaps she could.

Susan trusted she didn't look as apprehensive as she felt. She'd told herself, and Carly, again and again this was not a date. Yet, staying here, opposite Philip in this heartfelt cafe, sure felt like a date. Furthermore, perhaps it was simply living in fantasy land on her part, however she really struggled to be sure whether Philip felt the same way. A few times, she'd discovered him gazing at her mouth. From the get go, he'd rapidly turned away. However, as the night went on, he'd look his fill and afterward nonchalantly shift his thoughtfulness regarding her eyes. Also, sweet child Jesus! It was absolutely impossible that she could misjudge the intensity and want in his eyes. She'd then unwittingly — indeed, frankly, most likely intentionally — lick her lips, and his eyes would get back to her mouth.

Susan was totally turned on. Her alveolars solidified and she crossed and uncrossed her legs in a pointless endeavor to lighten the throb in her center. Presence of mind flew through the window, and the sum of everything on her mind was making wild, energetic love with this man. Which made her ponder the times they'd been together previously. As a young fellow, Mack had been a unimaginably capable sweetheart. Her heart accelerated when she envisioned what having intercourse with Mack now. Dear Master. She probably won't make due. However, what a nice job!

She didn't know whether she was feeling better or not when Philip dealt with the bill and the two of them got up to leave. Her legs shuddered and her underwear were at that point clammy. At the point when he set his hand on her lower back to direct her out of the eatery, she quickly envisioned that hand on her bosom, between her legs or in her hair, delicately directing her head down to —

"Susan?"

Susan woke up from her diversion to provocative town and acknowledged Philip was hanging tight for her to get in his truck. She moved in and took a few full breaths while Philip strolled around to the driver's side. When he was in and had turned over the motor, Susan contacted Philip's hand and said, "Thank you for this evening. I made some exquisite memories."

He peered down where her hand laid on his and tenderly grabbed hold. With his eyes consuming into hers, he lifted her hand to his lips and kissed softly. "I'm happy," he said. "So did I."

He kept on holding just her hand, even while moving out of the parking area. Susan couldn't recall the last time a man had held her hand. It was great. Neither of them talked returning. There wasn't a need. It had been like that between them previously. On occasion, they'd had parcels to say. Also, different times, they'd been alright with the quietness and simply being together. After all the anguish and years between them, they'd figured out how to find that once more.

At the point when they showed up at her home, Philip strolled her to her front entryway. She wanted to request that he come inside and afterward see where that drove. However, before she could ask, Philip inclined down and talked delicately into her ear.

"You asked before assuming I might want to come inside. Ask me once more."

Her breath hitched in her throat and she replied, "Might you want to come inside?"

"More than I need to inhale," Philip answered, his voice unpleasant.

Susan turned, hands shudder, and endeavored to open the entryway. At the point when she felt Mack's lips brush across the rear of her neck, she nearly dropped the keys. After two fruitless endeavors to embed the critical in the handle, Philip's hand covered her shudder one to direct the key into the space. When they were both inside, Philip pulled her to him and kissed her. She dropped her handbag and keys and raised up her arms to circle his neck as she squeezed herself closer.

Feelings and sensations overflowed her desire filled mind as Philip desolated her mouth with his. At the point when he delivered her mouth and ran his lips along the bend of her neck, she turned her head to permit him better access, while her fingers went through his hair. His mouth got back to catch hers again as his hands slid down her back to cup her behind. His knees adapted to take on her weight and when he lifted her, she immediately folded her legs over his abdomen. Feeling the hardness of his great erection against her pussy, she purposely scoured herself this way and that against him. This brought a long, low groan from his lips as he squeezed kisses along her jaw.

In the following second, he put her down on the love seat and his weight on her followed. Presently, with one hand at the rear of her head, his other was allowed to meander. His thumb brushed over her bosom and waited to rub delicately against her alveolar. She needed to cry when she understood the dress she went gaga for was not made for a love seat make-out meeting. The neck area was not adequately low to free her bosom. However, Philip ended up being an incredible issue solver. He inclined away somewhat so he could snatch the fix of her dress, and afterward raised it until her bra was uncovered. He took care of the back catch with his other hand, and the hostile underwear was as of now not a hindrance. He paused for a minute to see the value in the sight. His finger swiped over the solidified stub and he murmured, "So gorgeous," before his lips encompassed her alveolar.

Susan experienced the glow of his mouth, delicate nip of his teeth and the most scrumptious, cadenced pulls as he licked and sucked at initial one bosom, then, at that point, the other. She wanted him. Inside her. Presently.

Her hands bungled down his body so she could detach his jeans. After a few endeavors, the button gave way and she started to slide down his zipper. Before she had the option to free his rooster, his hand arrived at down to stop her.

"Philip," she asked. "If it's not too much trouble."

"Susan, we can't. I have no condoms."

Tossing a container of cold water on her would have had similar impact as his words.

"What?" she asked, trusting she'd misread him.

"I have no condoms with me. I didn't anticipate — I didn't design on…this."

As Susan battled to think and fix her breathing, she recalled how they'd moved beyond this specific impediment before. "We didn't necessarily have condoms in secondary school," she said as she moved alluringly under him.

Philip's grin told her he recalled every one of the imaginative ways they'd figured out how to satisfy each other in those days. "No, we didn't."

Susan's finger languidly followed the diagram of Philip's lips. "For what reason don't we proceed with this in the room?"

When they entered her room, Philip took care of freeing Hannah of her dress and undies. As she remained before him, totally bare, she didn't feel humiliated or reluctant by any means. How is that possible? Such a lot of time had passed by since they'd been together this way. Be that as it may, this felt so right. Like a piece of her had been feeling the loss of such a long time, and no measure of outrage and grief she'd had could diminish her affection toward him. She didn't have any idea where this would lead. He hadn't referenced anything about remaining.

Thus, she'd quite recently live at the time. Also, stress over the results later.

"Yet again you have too many garments on," she mumbled, her hand floating down to his somewhat open zipper. This time, he permitted her to go on until all his garments were disposed of on the floor.

As they stood confronting one another, Philip measured her face in his grasp and said, voice breaking, "I've missed you so freaking a lot."

With her heart detonating with feeling, Susan hurled herself in his arms and kissed him. Folding his arms over her and lifting, he gradually strolled to the bed and put her down her delicately. Susan shut her eyes at the scrumptious feel of him when he let himself down, taking consideration to not squash her with his full weight.

Presently, she thought, he's at last home.

Philip needed to kick himself for not being ready. He'd ensure he was at absolutely no point ever without a condom in the future. He'd needed just to sink down into Susan's body and watch her face as he siphoned all through her, bringing them both to an incredible delivery. However, being together this way? It felt more close. What's more, not set in stone to give Susan as much joy as possible. In this way, he took as much time as necessary at Susan's sweet lips, nipping at her mouth and afterward calming the keep quiet. He hesitantly left her mouth and squeezed kisses over her face and neck, and gradually worked his direction down her chest. As his mouth approached her bosoms, her alveolars turned out to be much harder, as though they were asking for his consideration. He kissed and licked each bosom softly to prod and torment her. He grinned when she at last snatched his head and held his mouth to her bosom. Showing compassion for her, he brought one alveolar into his mouth, concerned it with his tongue and afterward sucked. Hard. Susan shouted out and angled her back. He sucked more enthusiastically and afterward substituted his considerations between each bosom. His hand slid down her paunch to her pussy.

"OK, child. You're so fucking wet." He dunked one finger into her opening and afterward tenderly scoured her clit.

"Please, Philip. Please," was Hannah's frantic reaction as she raised her pelvis, looking for more erosion.

"I have you, child," Mack murmured. He expanded the strain of his fingers on her clit and continued sucking her alveolar.

Hannah's cries and groans expanded as she approached her delivery. Unexpectedly, her body went firm and shivers wracked her. Mack proceeded with serious areas of strength for him on her alveolar all through her climax. When her body quieted and she was breathing intensely, his mouth left her bosom.

He smoothed her hair away from her face and looked as she gradually descended from the high of her delivery. With one last full breath, she woke up.

"Goodness," she murmured.

He was unable to help himself. He inclined down and squeezed a delicate, virtuous kiss all the rage.

"When I slow down and rest, I'll give back," she expressed, arriving at up to put her arms around his neck.

"You don't need to do anything, child. I'm great simply realizing I gave you joy." Shockingly, Philip understood this was the unadulterated fact of the matter. He'd never need to cause Susan to feel committed to perform such a cozy demonstration. Regardless of whether they'd exactly the same thing previously. Besides, he truly had no clue about where they remained with one another now, since they'd bounced solidly into the vibe great stuff without examining the standards first.

Susan's eyebrows went up. "Truly?"

Before Philip could reply, Susan bent with the goal that she was on top peering down at him. "Thus, what you're talking about is that you wouldn't believe I should do this?" She'd arrived at down and taken his rooster in her grasp, siphoning all over a couple of times. "You couldn't care for that?"

Philip needed to focus to hold his eyes back from moving back in his mind. "No, I just implied you don't need to — fuck!"

Susan had slid down and taken him in her mouth. The blend of warmth, wetness and her tongue vacillating over him was sufficiently to send him past the brink. What's more, despite the fact that he had the option to keep down this time, he realized he wouldn't save control for a really long time. This forecast confirmed when only a couple of moments later, he detonated. His climax came over him like a cargo train, shivers racking his body for what appeared until the end of time. At the point when he recovered his detects, he saw Susan checking out at him with an extremely conceited and fulfilled smile. He started to grin back and afterward he understood what he'd recently finished. Method for going there, Philip. You tell her she doesn't have to do that to you, and what do you do? Besides the fact that you come in her mouth yet you don't have the respectability to caution her. Asshole.

He cleaned his face with his hands, moaned and said, "I am so grieved."

As she shifted her head with disarray, Susan answered, "For?"

"For what simply occurred. I didn't — You shouldn't — "

Susan facilitated forward and afterward swung one leg over Philip so she rode him. She inclined down until they were nearly nose to nose. "You gave me delight and I gave you joy. I realize it's been some time for me, yet I sort of believed that is the manner by which this should go. I didn't feel committed to do anything." She delicately kissed his lips. "I needed to."

Philip gestured and felt somewhat ludicrous for bringing it up. With a grin, he said, "I'm happy."

They smiled at one another briefly until Hannah turned away and afterward leisurely got up and off the bed. She caught a robe that was holding tight a snare on the rear of her entryway and rapidly tied the belt. Keeping away from his eyes now, she inquired, "Anyway, you're making a beeline for Houston tomorrow, isn't that so? What time would you say you are intending to leave?"

Bastard. That's what he'd disregarded. "Not genuine early, I don't think. There's no set time I should be back. Consider the possibility that I make an appearance at the bistro on out. So I can see you again before I leave."

Susan grinned and gestured. "I'd like that."

Philip attempted to put a finger on his present status of psyche. He'd assumed he'd be feeling better to return to his home and occupation at long last. He'd assumed he'd blow into town, cover Straightforward and afterward blow right back out. He'd at no point ever envisioned he'd accompany Susan in the future. Also, presently? He would have rather not left her again. In any case, he had liabilities.

"Hello," he said delicately. "Come here briefly." He'd moved to sit on the bed and tapped the space close to him for Susan to sit. He measured her jaw and got her eyes. "I need to return to my work. However, I will invest for a few excursion effort and I'll be back around Thanksgiving. We'll have additional time then to talk. About us." He kissed the side of her mouth. "Since I particularly maintain that there should be an 'us.'"

She arrived at up to put her hand over his. "I'd like that to."

While Philip was intellectually high-fin' himself over her affirmation, he saw the smart look all over. "What?" Philip inquired.

Susan shrugged and expressed, "Sort of unexpected that Peter Brownsville was answerable for destroying us and uniting us back. Wouldn't you say?"

I believe that is the main nice thing he could possibly do for me. "Better believe it. I see the incongruity there. I say, we should simply go with it." Remorsefully, Philip noticed the time and realized Susan must be at the bistro early tomorrow. With one final kiss, he guaranteed her he'd see her the following morning.

Six

Chapter 6

Susan checked the time for the 100th time. Try not to overreact, Susan. He presumably chose to stay in bed. Not every person gets up at four o'clock each day. He said he'd be here.

She'd showed up at the bistro as early as possible as expected in light of the fact that Sunday mornings were occupied with numerous families coming in for breakfast either previously or after chapel. She hadn't anticipated that Philip should come by when she originally opened, yet it was right around nine o'clock now. Perhaps he returned to the house to accomplish some more work. Perhaps he ran into somebody he knew and forgot about the time. There must be a valid justification. Since he said he'd be here.

Susan was shocked to see Mrs. Hodges stroll in and sit down.

Catching a menu from the counter, Hannah advanced over to the more seasoned lady's table.

"Good day, Mrs. H. I'm astounded to see you toward the beginning of today. You normally don't stop in when you have visitors at the B&B." Susan consequently put down an espresso mug and snatched the warm carafe to fill it with espresso.

"All things considered, my main visitor was gone when I got up toward the beginning of today at five. Thus, in the wake of stripping the cloths and cleaning the washroom, I chose to indulge myself with an aiding of your morning meal goulash."

Susan glared. "Philip was gone before you got up toward the beginning of today?"

Mrs. Hodges blended sugar into her espresso and gestured. "Indeed, he had said he wanted to leave today. I simply didn't understand he implied before dawn. He was sufficiently circumspect to pass on the way to his room open so I'd realize he was no more."

"I'll, um, go put your request in," Susan said absently. She felt both tipsy and debilitated to her stomach. In the wake of conveying the request to the kitchen, she looked for asylum in the administrative center. She shut the entryway and rested up against it. You're simply going overboard. There's presumably an entirely valid justification why he left before dawn and hasn't tried to call or stop by. Not set in stone to demonstrate that she didn't have anything to stress over, she pulled her telephone from her pocket and viewed as Philip's number. Before she lost her nerve, she called. It went directly to voice message. He most likely went by the house to do a few somewhat late things and reached out. He likely left his telephone in his truck. There's nothing more to it. Or…maybe he was working at the house and hurt himself. Perhaps he's oblivious and needs clinical consideration.

Susan snatched her satchel out of her work area and strolled back to the kitchen. "Cathy, I really want to leave for a couple of moments. Could you at any point deal with everything here for some time? I ought not be excessively lengthy."

Before Cathy got an opportunity to say anything, Susan was out the entryway and in her vehicle. Consider the possibility that Philip was truly stung. He truly ought not be there working without anyone else. It simply wasn't protected. As she drove, Susan intellectually inspected every last bit of her medical aid preparing as well as the bit by bit process for CPR.

That was all in vain when she didn't see Philip's truck anyplace at the Brownsville estate. She sat in her vehicle for a couple of moments and attempted to deal with everything her cerebrum held saying to her. Philip hadn't arrived. He left early toward the beginning of today without bidding farewell. Once more.

She felt like a dolt. She'd trusted him. Is it true that he was that difficult up for a little activity? With his attractive features and appeal, she didn't trust that briefly. Perhaps he simply needed to do a past love interest for poops and chuckles prior to going to his life in Houston. Perhaps he was very much like all the other people who in every case left her. But he'd left her two times.

As her heart went to stone, Susan pivoted to go to the bistro. As she passed Carly's condo, she saw Carly's vehicle in the parking area and immediately turned in. At the point when Carly opened her entryway, her invite grin immediately went to a scowl when she saw the vibe of complete obliteration all over.

"Goodness, honey!" Carly quickly enveloped her companion in an embrace. "What occurred?"

Susan's lip shuddered as she said, "He left me once more."

Carly directed Hannah inside and drove her to her parlor lounge chair. "OK," she said. "Let me know what occurred."

Susan related the occasions of her date with Philip and all that happened later. The more she talked, however, the angrier she got.

"You know, I thought he needed to reunite. I thought he was true. In any case, I get it was all a game to him. Somewhat fun with the pathetic and frantic young lady he knew from secondary school." Susan cleaned her face and put on a decided look all over. "I won't allow him the opportunity to rehash that to me. I'm finished with Philip Brownsville."

"Are you certain he didn't leave you a message or message you?" Carly inquired.

"I've checked. Nothing. What's more, I even attempted to call him. Went directly to voice message. I won't burn through anything else of my valuable time or energy on that man. I can't." Susan remained strong with a reestablished feeling of assurance. "I will return to the bistro and go about my business. I will not allow him to slow down my life once more. I suppose one of us didn't grow up all things considered."

Carly gave Susan a major embrace. "Everything being equal, I was pulling for you. I'd truly trusted things would have worked out between both of you."

Susan gave her a miserable grin. "No doubt, all things considered, I surmise we were both off-base."

Philip was depleted WAS . Since getting back to Houston, he'd made due on unadulterated adrenaline. Until further notice, Ryan had been updated from basic to serious. His accomplice wasn't in the clear yet, yet he basically had a decent opportunity at recuperation now, as long as he encountered no significant misfortunes.

In the event that the medical caretakers didn't compose the ongoing day on the message board in the room, Philip wouldn't understand what day it was. He shut his eyes and inclined his head back against the wall. All that had occurred since he'd addressed that 2:00 a.m. call had been one unmitigated mess after another. One moment, he'd been dreaming about Susan and the following, he'd been tossing his poo in a bag and hustling out to his truck. In his flurry to get his stuff stacked and get out and about, he probably dropped his telephone. He enigmatically set it on the hood while he put his gear in the truck. It was doubtlessly broken out and about somewhere close to Honey Springs and Houston.

He'd gone directly to the emergency clinic and he'd been there from that point forward. Basically everybody from the region had been by to mind Ryan as well as others from adjoining areas. There's been a consistent progression of individuals over the course of the day and the majority of the evening. Everybody on the power knew that, in a matter of seconds, they could be lying in an emergency clinic bed. Or on the other hand in the mortuary.

This was the main night that it had been somewhat calm. Which implied Philip had an opportunity to think. Which implied he pondered Susan and the last point he'd made to her. Fuck. Without his telephone, he wasn't ready to basically send her a fast message to make sense of for what reason he'd left so unexpectedly. Right now, he liked to make sense of face to face. He could hardly comprehend what she should think and his heart sank. She'd see once he told her the purposes for his unexpected flight. Isn't that so? He was depending on it. They had begun something. Also, he expected to see where it would go.

Dread had held him back from chasing after any sort of long haul relationship. Dread that he would turn into his dad. In any case, in the wake of seeing Ryan scarcely sticking onto life, he started reconsidering his future. Ryan had no family and had likewise kept away from any committed relationships. If not for his companions and colleagues, he'd have been here without anyone else. Philip didn't need that for his future. He needed to impart his life to somebody. The great times and the terrible.

He adored his work in policing. Regulation officials had saved his life. From getting away from his harmful dad to assisting him with turning into the man he was intended to be. In any case, the occupation was not helpful for keeping a solid, cherishing relationship. He worked extended periods of time and saw things that spooky his fantasies.

Philip's contemplation were interfered with by Ryan's developments. Philip stood and ventured nearer so he could talk delicately to his companion and accomplice. "Hello, man. You about to rest constantly? Fella, you realize you feel weak at the knees over medical caretakers. You're passing up a major opportunity. For sure."

Ryan's eyelids shuddered a couple of times lastly lifted, only a break. There were still so many things that could turn out badly, yet Philip said a speedy supplication of gratitude for the positive sign. "In the event that you're pondering, you strolled into an arrangement. The uplifting news? You figured out how to take out Rostropovich and two of his men. The main person to leave that rear entryway is singing like a bird. In any case, man. You not hanging tight for me to return to set up the meet? Not cool."

Ryan replied by lifting his center finger somewhat. Philip got the move and chuckled. "No doubt, I know. I presumably would have done likewise."

Ryan's mouth jerked somewhat before he shut his eyes. At the point when Philip was persuaded Ryan was resting, he moved back and got back to his seat to proceed with his vigil.

Thanksgiving day was predictable for Hannah. Her folks had come in before in the week and they'd cooked and snickered and eaten throughout the week. They'd made arrangements to get together with some RV companions to head out down to Mississippi and invest some energy along the Bay Coast. They'd had all the typical Thanksgiving charge on Wednesday so they could start off bright and early Thursday morning. Along these lines, at 7:00 a.m. on Thanksgiving morning, Susan thought of herself as alone.

She'd been so bustling in the weeks since Philip had left, once more, without a word, that she had opportunity and willpower to harp on the circumstance. She arranged heaps of additional dishes during this season. Her shoemakers and pumpkin pies were extremely famous, and a significant number of her clients mentioned them for their own family dinners. In this way, there was additional heating up and time in the bistro, which was a much needed diversion now. Yet, today, the bistro was shut. She thought about 1,000,000 things she could finish around the house today, however all things considered, she constructed a fire in the chimney, fixed some her number one cinnamon-seasoned espresso, and settled down on the lounge chair with the most recent romance book she'd got from the pharmacy. Perusing sentiment was her gift to herself. She adored following the couple on their excursion to their joyfully ever later. She was a heartfelt on a fundamental level and despite the fact that she hadn't found her blissful completion, she actually had trust. No doubt, Susan. You continue to let yourself know that. You need Philip. What's more, just Philip. Things haven't worked out with different men in your day to day existence. Why would that be? Perhaps you knew from the start they weren't what or who you needed.

Lost in her viewpoints, she didn't hear the truck drive up. The thumps on her entryway frightened her and she immediately put down her espresso. She perceived Philip's truck when she peered through the window. She promptly eased back her means, approaching the entryway, however not opening it.

"Susan. It's Philip. Kindly open the entryway. I really want to converse with you — make sense of where I've been. I — kindly open the entryway. If it's not too much trouble."

She connected with turn the door handle and afterward halted herself. How frequently would you say you will succumb to his untruths? How often would you say you will allow him to utilize you?

Philip thumped on the entryway once more. "Susan. I realize I hurt you. In any case, I guarantee, I can make sense of."

Unfit to stop herself, she glanced through the peephole. His appearance stunned her. His face was pale and worn down and she was almost certain he'd shed pounds. He didn't look presumptuous or self-important. He looked thumped and… tired. Before she could work herself out of it once more, she opened the entryway.

Philip turned upward and grinned, his face confident. "Hello.

Much obliged to you for opening the entryway. If it's not too much trouble, could I at any point come in so we can talk?"

Without saying a word, she ventured back and motioned for him to enter. She shut the entryway and afterward strolled into the kitchen. She didn't need the closeness of the front room sofa. She topped off her espresso mug and inquired, "Could you like some espresso?"

"Indeed, I would. Much obliged to you." Philip remained at the table until Susan put his cup down. He sat after Susan sat down. She looked as he took a taste and grinned in appreciation.

"I nearly failed to remember what great espresso possesses a flavor like. I thought nothing was more awful than area break room espresso. Yet, that was before I had clinic espresso. This? This resembles fluid paradise." He took another taste.

Susan's heart skirted a thump. "Clinic espresso?"

"That Saturday night, after our date, I got a call at two o'clock that morning. My accomplice, Ryan, had been shot and was in basic condition." Philip stopped and gulped hard prior to proceeding. "They didn't know whether he'd make it until morning. I expected to get to the clinic. Quick. While hustling to get my packs in the truck, I lost my telephone." He halted to take one more swallow of his espresso. "At the point when I got to the medical clinic, everything was insane. Loads of disarray and individuals dropping by. Ryan was still in a medical procedure." Philip ran a hand through his hair and moaned. "I drove directly to the emergency clinic from here and I didn't leave until that one weekend from now, but to run home and shower. Ryan has no family and I would have rather not let him there be."

In the wake of hearing his story, Susan couldn't help herself. She contacted touch Philip's hand. "How's your companion now? Is it safe to say that he will be alright?"

Philip promptly enclosed Susan's hand in his. "He has a ton of recuperating to do, yet he's gained a ton of headway. His anticipation is great."

Susan grinned. "That is great. I'm happy he will be alright."

At the point when Susan attempted to pull her hand back, Mack's hold fixed.

"Please accept my apologies. I realize you most likely figured the most obviously terrible when I didn't make it by that next morning." Philip shook his head in disdain. "It appears I'm continuously saying 'sorry' to you for something. I simply trust you can track down it in your heart to excuse me once more."

As she investigated his face, Susan needed to concede he appeared to be genuine. His story was conceivable. She envisioned she would have responded likewise on the off chance that she'd been informed Carly, Lucy or Sara was in the emergency clinic and not expected to get by. "Obviously, I pardon you. You expected to get back at the earliest opportunity to keep an eye on your companion."

Philip breathed out and his body noticeably loose. "Much obliged to you. I will give my all to make it dependent upon you. I know it's Thanksgiving night and there presumably aren't many spots open, however I'd very much want to take you out to supper tomorrow evening. I could pick — "

"Philip," Hannah interfered. She nibbled her lip. "I, uh, acknowledged your statement of regret so we're great there. But…as far as there being anything more between us…I simply don't have any idea." She figured out how to facilitate her hand from his.

Seven

Chapter 7

Philip's most memorable nature was to overreact. Perhaps ask. In any case, he realized Susan was attempting to safeguard herself. She was hesitant to trust him once more. He'd simply need to ensure she had no more motivations to uncertainty him. Or then again his goals. He'd had a great deal of time to think while sitting next to Ryan's clinic bed. Life was short. Also, he needed to pack all of living he could into whatever amount of time he had. He believed a lady should return home to each evening. He needed a family. Kids. He needed everything. Obviously, all of that terrified him. Be that as it may, he trusted everything will work out just fine. He needed all of that with the lady sitting opposite him. Furthermore, in that exact moment, he saw everything. He would be patient and get it going.

"You have a long list of motivations to feel as such. It makes perfect sense to me. Be that as it may, I might want to ask you to simply allow me an opportunity to demonstrate you can trust me. We'll go as delayed as need might arise. I simply need to invest energy with you. Get to know you as you are today. Furthermore, for you to get to know me. As a man. What do you say?"

Philip watched Susan's face intently, unwittingly pausing his breathing. Susan bit her lip and glared, and a bunch of feelings streaked in her eyes. He did a psychological clench hand siphon when she said, "OK. Be that as it may, I can't make you any commitments about...us."

Philip shook his head. "I need no commitments. I simply need to get to know each other. I will be visiting the area for the rest of the year. I truly haven't gotten some much needed rest since I've been with the office, and presently appeared to be as great a period as any. I've chosen to keep the house and land. Basically for the time being. There's still a ton of work to do, however I might want to take you out some time. Perhaps go out to eat. Or on the other hand we could simply remain in and watch a film."

"That sounds decent. You're remaining at the B&B once more?" Susan asked as she got up to get more espresso for both herself and Mack.

"That was the arrangement. However, Mr. Hodges called me last week and let me know they've been disapproving of the water lines, and they needed to drop every one of their reservations until the fixes are made. Thus, I'll simply remain at the house. I brought a little generator and a hiking bed."

Susan grimaced. "Generator? There's no power there?"

"The utilities had been stopped some time back. Before I have everything associated once more, I need to ensure the wiring is great. Thus, until I can get a circuit tester out there to look at everything, I would rather not possibility torching the spot."

Susan kept on grimacing yet before she could pose another inquiry, he said, "I didn't contemplate you being occupied today. Am I holding you back from anything? Is it safe to say that you are anticipating your folks? Or on the other hand would you say you will have Thanksgiving with your companions?"

"In reality, Mother and Father left toward the beginning of today. They had plans to get together with one more couple in Tennessee. We had our Thanksgiving yesterday so they could start off bright and early. Lucy is still in Little Stone, and Carly is going through the day with her family in Lake Marten. Sara has a break from school yet she's functioning this week. I've gone through the most recent couple of weeks baking and cooking, so I will appreciate doing literally nothing today."

Philip would have rather not stayed around too long. Susan had excused him. That was a beginning. Presently, he simply had to demonstrate to her that she could trust him once more. He stood up and said, "Indeed, I'll go. I have a lot of stuff I want to finish today. Much obliged to you for pardoning me. Once more. I'm certain you have a great deal of 'nothing' to begin on, so I'll just — "

"How about you stay here all things being equal?" Susan's words came out rapidly, like she expected to rush and make the idea before she altered her perspective.

The proposition totally caught off-guard him. "I…uh…I value the proposition. In any case, I could never exploit you like that. That is not why I came by." Philip was moved by her idea. What's more, truly, now that he mulled over everything, it was the very sort of act of kindness Susan would make.

Susan stood up and put her hands on her hips. "Yet, you can't remain in that house like that. I have a lot of room here. You can remain in one of the extra rooms. I'll stress over you in that house with no power, or intensity or water. If it's not too much trouble. It would cheer me up." The vibe of worry, alongside a solid portion of assurance, was scratched all over. "Presently, go get your stuff and acquire it."

"Much obliged to you." He tenderly maneuvered her into his arms and gave her an embrace, cautious to keep the contact in the companion to-companion class. He gave his all to overlook the vibe of her warm, delicate body against his and ventured back before he truly needed to. They should have been companions first. Then, at that point, ideally, they could continue on toward something else.

He recovered his bag from his truck and followed Susan down the passage to the extra room. When he went into the room, he was assaulted with recollections. This had been Susan's room in secondary school. He gazed at the bed. Despite the fact that it wasn't the very twin bed that had been in here previously, he thought about every one of the times he and Susan sat on her bed and chipped away at schoolwork tasks. Once in a while, he'd figured out how to sneak a little kiss. Besides the fact that he recollected those sweet times, yet he likewise contemplated how blissful he was simply to be in a home with guardians who wouldn't hesitate to show love to one another or to Hannah. It was a spot Philip had felt appreciated and acknowledged.

Philip grinned and shook his head. "I sort of expected to see the pink and purple unsettle quilt."

Susan snickered. "Definitely, I felt weak at the knees over pink and purple in those days. Fortunately, my enlivening preferences have turned into somewhat more refined."

The two of them took a gander at one another briefly, and afterward Philip made a sound as if to speak and said, "I would be wise to get moving on the off chance that I desire to finish anything today. Much obliged once more. I'm happy we can be companions."

He strolled toward the entryway and afterward convoluted. "I practically neglected." He pulled his telephone from his pocket. "I got another telephone. Do you mind giving me your number once more?"

"I wouldn't fret by any means." She presented the number as Philip entered the data in his contacts. "Simply message me and I'll save your number too."

"Sounds great. I'll surrender you a heads when I'm prepared to return."

As he fired up his truck and retreated from the carport, he had an immense grin all over.

Susan watched Philip drive away and afterward presented herself with one more mug of espresso. She didn't know how she had an outlook on her greeting for him to remain with her. She realized it had been the correct thing to do. Despite all that had occurred between them, she just couldn't walk out on him. Indeed, she'd been crushed when he'd left without a word quite a while back. Be that as it may, she wasn't floundering in hopelessness from that point forward. As a matter of fact, up to this point, she hadn't really thought about him by any stretch of the imagination. He'd made sense of why he needed to leave. The twice. What's more, she got it and concurred that he didn't have a decision either time. In any case, that didn't mean she was up for greater frustration and grief.

They could be companions. Correct? They were both mature grown-ups. Since they'd been frantically enamored with one another in secondary school didn't mean they couldn't keep a dispassionate relationship now. Correct? Things weren't precisely 'dispassionate' between us half a month prior. In all decency, that one little blunder occurred subsequent to figuring out that he'd been manhandled. Feelings had been high and… well, things went somewhat crazy. Yet, they were past that at this point. Philip would remain at her home for a brief period until remaining in his own home was protected. Everything would have been okay.

Susan completed her espresso and essentially avoided a few doors down. She cherished special times of year and was dependably anxious to start finishing for Christmas. By late evening, she'd set up and designed her Christmas tree and chimney mantle, hung wreaths, and set out candles, Christmas cushions, and Christmas focal points on the lounge area, anteroom, and end tables. Indeed, she had a counterfeit tree. It was such a ton simpler to set up and bring down, particularly since she was all alone. She wrapped up outside by hanging sparkle lights on the patio railings and putting two little shrubbery trees by the front entryway.

Taking a gander at the time, she was shocked to see that it was late evening as of now. Her considerations went to supper and what she ought to eat. She guessed she could simply have another turkey sandwich, yet that held no allure. Foreboding shadows were working toward the north, and she recollected the conjecture called for downpour and colder temperatures with the methodology of a virus front. Something hot and good would truly stir things up around town. And afterward she knew precisely very thing she'd make. Turkey pot pie.

Subsequent to making the pie covering, she began the filling of turkey, vegetables and a rich, smooth sauce. Similarly as she put the pie in the stove, the downpour started. While hanging tight for it to complete the process of baking, Susan did a heap of clothing and went online to cover a few bills. Similarly as she got done, her telephone dinged with a message from Philip.

"On my way. Be there in a couple."

She checked the pie and the outside was an ideal brilliant brown.

She took it out and put it to the side to rest. Then, before she could stop herself, she went to her room and changed out of her agreeable warm up pants and slipped on her #1 pants. She was unable to help it assuming that her number one pants made her butt look incredible. That is the reason they were her number one. Presently, her old, oversize Shirt looked odd with the pants, so she pulled it over her head and supplanted it with a delicate, fitted wool shirt. Furthermore, before she could stop herself, she checked her hair in the restroom reflect and ran a fast brush through it and added a slim layer of mascara to her eyelashes. That is the point at which she started contending with herself.

What's going on with you? What? For what reason do you tend to think about what you resemble? You told Philip you would have rather not been everything except companions. Since you put on clean garments. Furthermore, brush your hair. Furthermore, put on mascara would mean you not like to be more than companions, senseless. Definitely. Right. You don't trust me? No. I don't actually. Since when he contacts you, you actually get goose pimples. So? It's November. You're simply cold. That is not it by any stretch of the imagination. You actually need him. You actually need the fantasy. Things being what they are, how often would you say you will allow him to hurt you? Leave you? Dishearten you? There's no adoration without risk. What's more, he merits the gamble?

As she remained there before the mirror, Susan pondered that last inquiry. Was Philip worth the gamble to her heart? She accepted he was. In some cases, the heart needs what the heart needs. She'd needed him as a little kid. What's more, she needed him as a lady. She would have rather not denied herself of the opportunity that the situation would work out with Philip. Indeed, he lived in another state. Be that as it may, certain individuals had the option to make far-removed relationships work. She'd keep a receptive outlook and remain hopeful. Since, where it counts, that is what her identity was. Furthermore, with that, she went after the lipstick also.

Philip had his hand up to thump when the entryway opened and he was eye to eye with Susan. Jesus. How could he should stay faithful to his commitment to simply be companions when she seemed to be that? Perhaps he ought to simply get his stuff and go stay at his home. In any case, on the off chance that his objective was for them to get to know one another, he expected to endure it here. Something let him know he would have been investing a ton of energy in the shower.

"I trust you're ravenous," Susan said, her hand gently contacting his chest.

Remain cool, he told himself. She's simply being well disposed.

"I'm," he answered truly.

"How about you go get tidied up, and afterward we can eat," she proposed.

"Good thought," Philip concurred rapidly and strolled to his room. His longing for Susan was abrogating all of his sound judgment. In the event that he knew worse, he'd swear she was playing with him. Yet, that was insane in light of the fact that she was the person who demanded they must be companions. So he probably envisioned the manner in which her hand waited on his chest and how her eyes appeared to be centered around his mouth. Perhaps his steady condition of excitement since seeing Susan today had confined the oxygen stream to his cerebrum. There was just a single method for helping his "issue" as of now.

He immediately peeled off his garments and ventured into the shower. In the wake of applying a liberal measure of cleanser to his hands, he arrived at down and grabbed hold of his rooster with one hand and put the other on the shower wall before him to prepare himself. As pictures of Susan streaked through his psyche, he worked his chicken increasingly fast until he tracked down his delivery. He remained there, head down, breathing intensely until his legs felt less anxious. He must stay at work longer than required to get his home wrapped up.

He wrapped cleaning up and afterward wearing some very much worn pants and a Shirt. At the point when he got to the doorway to the kitchen, he halted to respect the view. Susan was remaining at the counter, her back to him, and the sum total of his thoughts was the manner by which amazing her butt looked. Indeed, crap. His shower arrangement didn't work long by any means. He made a sound as if to speak and inquired, "Might I at any point assist you with anything?"

Susan investigated her shoulder and said happily, "You can get the pitcher of tea from the cooler and pour us each a glass."

Susan put the pie plate on the table and said, "I genuinely want to believe that you like pot pie. I made one from the remainder of the extra turkey."

"Amazing. It looks and scents delectable," Philip said truly.

Susan served him an enormous part and his mouth watered. In the wake of taking a nibble, he said, "This is remarkable. No big surprise you've made such a progress of your cafe. You have some distraught cooking abilities."

"I'm happy you like it. I've been considering putting a variant of this on the bistro menu."

"You ought to. It'd be a moment hit," Susan said between nibbles.

Susan grinned as she added one more serving to his plate. "Were you ready to finish a great deal today?" she asked, taking a taste of her beverage.

Philip glanced around and smiled. "Not however much I'd figured I would. Everything is agonizingly slow when there's such a huge amount to do, it's difficult to choose precisely where to begin. From the change here, I'd say that wasn't an issue for you today by any means."

Philip looked extremely satisfied with herself. "I sort of have enlivening down to a science. I have an arrangement and I stick to it loyally."

Philip contemplated his loft in Houston. "I even own no Christmas beautification," he said as he put the last chomp in his mouth.

At the point when he looked into, Philip was gazing at him, confounded. "You have no Christmas embellishments? How would you adorn your Christmas tree?"

Shrugging, he said, "I don't."

Susan's look changed from confounded to stunned. "You don't set up a tree for Christmas? Not so much as a tabletop one?"

"No, why? I live alone. I work a great deal and don't get numerous guests. If I have any desire to see a tree, I simply head toward Hank and Cart's home."

Yet again Susan's demeanor changed, however presently she looked near tears. "I surmise I didn't understand before exactly the way that by itself you've been such a long time."

The last thing he needed was for Susan to feel frustrated about him. She'd continuously had a major heart. It was something he'd been drawn to. Before and presently.

"Hello, could I tidy up the kitchen while you go get a film we can watch?" He stood and carried his plate to the sink.

She followed and said, "You wash. I'll stack. And afterward we'll both go choose something to watch."

"I'll wager you have a whole choice of Christmas themed films," he said as he washed and stacked the dishes.

She chuckled and said, "Maybe?"

Shaking his head and grinning, he said, "I had an inclination."

As he peered down at her, her eyes hitting the dance floor with giggling, he needed so seriously to kiss her grinning lips. At the point when she turned away, dried her hands and started strolling to the lounge, she brought back behind her, "I know the ideal film for this evening."

He giggled when he understood that the film playing was Deadly Weapon. This lady was totally great.

Eight

Chapter 8

No issues up until now, Susan thought as she sat on the love seat and glanced around. She'd made a point to lay everything out before by leaving boxes and compartments on the lounge room seats which left the sofa as the main seating accessible. She arranged herself just to one side of the center. After a short glance around, Philip sat on the lounge chair close to her. With light from the chimney, TV and Christmas tree, the room was set.

The main issue was that Philip appeared to be treating her craving to simply be companions in a serious way. She got up to recover the toss from the seat and intentionally sat nearer to Philip when she got back to the sofa. Twisting her decisive advantages over the love seat, she spread twisted her major advantages over the lounge chair and spread the toss across her lap while inclining toward Philip's side. She felt his body solidify in response to her closeness. She asked honestly, "You don't care either way if we cuddle a little? Like bygone eras?"

He gulped hard and said in a stressed voice, "Not by any stretch." He brought his arm around her shoulder and held her to him.

She truly gave no consideration to the film by any stretch of the imagination. She rested her head against Philip's chest and could hear his consistent pulses, despite the fact that it appeared they appeared to speed up and force about that time. Other than his arm around her shoulder, Philip took no other action to contact her. Darn it all. When all else fails, compromise is unavoidable. She got the remote and stopped the film. She went to confront him and said, "Please accept my apologies, however this isn't working for me."

Briefly, she saw what resembled alarm in his eyes. "Susan — "

"I would rather not be companions, Philip." She carried her hand to the side of his face and looked as he shut his eyes and bowed his head down.

"Kindly glance at me," she murmured. His eyes opened and they were disheartening and miserable. "I need to be your beginning and end. Your darling. Your accomplice. Your team promoter. Your — "

His mouth descended on hers before she could complete her discourse. She needed to lose herself in the stunning strain of his lips on hers. At the point when she brought her arms up to fold over his neck and pull him nearer to her, he unexpectedly moved back. She halted her expressions of dissent when she saw the serious feelings in his eyes.

He carried two hands to her face and said generally, "You should be certain, Susan. I left you a long time back when I didn't have a decision. Furthermore, again half a month prior due to obligation. I won't leave you once more. I can't. In this way, on the off chance that you feel somewhat skeptical about us. About this. We should discuss them now. Furthermore, figure that poop out." As though he was unable to help himself, he kissed her again until she was winded.

At the point when he raised his head, she said, "I've never been all the more certain of anything in my life." Her voice major areas of strength for was clear.

He talked while peppering light kisses over her face. "I planned to stay away. Like you inquired. Be that as it may, now…all wagers are off."

To feel his weight on her as he maneuvered her down the love seat was glorious. Also, when he settled his hips among hers and she felt his erection, the sum of everything on her mind was having him inside her and — "Philip! Pause!" she expressed, pushing at him and attempting to stand out enough to be noticed.

Philip appeared to battle to comprehend. "Susan? What — "

"Condoms," she relaxed. "I actually have no condoms." She needed to cry.

Philip snickered daintily. "Darling. I guaranteed myself after the keep going time we were on this love seat that I'd at absolutely no point ever be gotten ill-equipped in the future." He inclined down and kissed her nose. "I have a couple in my wallet."

Susan loosened up back on the lounge chair and said, "All things considered, all things considered, if it's not too much trouble, continue."

Rather than following her down, he stood up and accumulated her in his arms and lifted. "Could we carry on in the room since my wallet is there?" Without sitting tight for a response, he started strolling a few doors down.

Susan exploited her closeness to Philip's neck by kissing and gnawing during the excursion. He put her down on the bed, took the condoms out his wallet and put them on the bedside table. He sat on the bed and peered down at her.

"You're so damn gorgeous. How could I get so fortunate?" he murmured.

Susan held out her hands to urge Philip to rests with her. All things considered, he held her hands and maneuvered her into a sitting position. He kissed her daintily on the lips and afterward said, "You have too many garments on." He started to fix the buttons on her shirt until it was totally open and uncovered her sheer naked variety bra.

A sprinkle of a grin shaped all the rage and he said, "I recall you generally wore bras that fastened in the front in those days."

Susan grinned at the memory. "Definitely, indeed, that was the point at which we needed to take our minutes at whatever point we could and that saved a brief period, prior and then afterward. Yet, she said while running a finger across his lips, "we don't need to rush at this moment."

She needed to remain here, with Philip, as far as might be feasible. They hadn't even discussed a future and supposedly, he was exclusively here for the rest of the year. His work and home was in Houston. In any case, she'd take what she could get at this moment and stress over all of that later.

Philip peered down at Susan and gulped. "No," he concurred. "We don't have to rush. I need to take as much time as necessary and taste and kiss every last bit of your wonderful body. I need to make you shake with want. I need to feel you come while I'm inside you. And afterward, when you pause and rest, I believe should do everything over once more." He arrived at behind his neck and snatched his Shirt to pull it over his head. Bringing down his body over Susan, he kissed his direction from her lips to her bosoms, pampering them with consideration. This brought about the ideal impact. Susan wriggled and gasped, pushing her chest vertical while squeezing his head down to build the tension of his mouth on her alveolars.

His arrangements to take this sluggish were disentangling rapidly. As Susan's longing constructed, her hips push against his horrendously hard rooster in a rhythm that had him near the precarious edge of climax. His development away was met with a disappointed cry.

"Please, Philip! I'm soot close. I want — I want — "

"Shh, child. I understand what you want. I have you." As he talked, he slid down her body and started chipping away at the button and zipper of her pants. She contorted this way and that to assist him with working them over her hips and down her legs. Her underwear were straightaway.

She bent and attempted to come to the end table. "Condom," she said enthusiastically.

He held her legs to forestall her drawing nearer and said, "Not yet. I have something different as a primary concern first."

Susan dissented, "No, I need — Gracious! Yessed…"

The pleasantness of Sun's longing detonated in his mouth as he licked and sucked her clit. In the future, he'd take as much time as is needed and play and bother, however presently, he needed to make her come, quick and hard. From the manner in which her hips kicked up while her hands pushed down on his head, it wouldn't take long. With his center finger, he circumnavigated around her opening and pushed in leisurely. He pulled out it and afterward added his pointer. His tongue lapped at her clit in similar mood as his gradually siphoning fingers.

Under thirty seconds after the fact, she pulled his hair to the mark of agony, hardened and let out a high keening cry. Then, at that point, as though a switch had been switched off, her body loose and she was breathing intensely. Her hands, still in his hair, shuddered and jolted from tangible post-quake tremors.

He climbed to situate himself close to her and afterward brought her around to lie on top of him, getting her face into his neck and embracing her to him firmly. At long last, her breathing eased back and she got her head to check out at him with half-lidded eyes and a fulfilled grin. One of her hands floated down the side of his body and she glared.

"For what reason do you actually have your jeans on?"

Philip ran his give over the bend of Hannah's base.

"Since, without the jeans, we would have been finished after the initial fifteen minutes," he said with a smile. "Also, I needed to ensure I dealt with you first."

"Well," Susan expressed, sliding down the length of his body. "You've positively done that. Presently, I believe it's the ideal opportunity for me to deal with you." She worked at the button and zipper of his pants, however she halted to rub her hands over his erection first. His stomach muscles contracted and he petitioned God for control. He was on the edge and it wouldn't take a lot to push him over. Gradually, she worked his jeans down until she had the option to pull them off totally. He looked as she took his chicken in her grasp and contacted the tip of her tongue to the shimmering globule of semen at the tip. She viewed at him as she took him totally in her mouth. He shut his eyes and extended his head back, looking for the solidarity to fight the temptation to come. After a couple of additional strokes of her tongue, he was nearly at the final turning point.

"Susan," he croaked out as his hands went to her face. "Kindly stop. I would rather not come in your mouth and I'm ridiculously close." His leg muscles were shaking from his fight to keep down his delivery.

He was feeling significantly better when she sat up and held out her hand.

"Condom, please."

He hung over and snatched one from the end table. Subsequent to giving it to her, he prepared himself for a delayed meeting of we should perceive how-long-Susan-can-torment Philip-while-she-puts-the-condom-on-him. Shockingly, she was all business and the deed was finished with an insignificant measure of waiting touches.

Philip rode him and inclined down to kiss his lips, long and slow.

"Could you take over from here?" she murmured, scouring her nose along his.

Philip folded his arms over Susan and sat up. She squeaked with shock however the sound was removed when his mouth dove down on hers for a hard, wet kiss. He pulled away unexpectedly and lifted her up so his mouth

He stopped briefly to permit her to conform to him, and afterward he started to siphon his hips in sluggish, profound strokes. He attempted to contemplate unremarkable, moronic poo since, in such a case that he focused a lot on exactly the way in which fucking great it felt to be back inside Susan, he wouldn't make it past the sixty-second imprint. In any case, he tragically looked at her. They were dubiously glossy and loaded up with such a lot of feeling he lost his cadence, however at that point immediately changed. They kept on investigating each other's eyes as he expanded the speed of his strokes. He arrived at down between their bodies and applied strain with his thumb to her clit. Her hips countered the tension and soon, her inward muscles were grasping around his rooster, bringing him past the brink too.

At the point when he was capable, Philip got up and discarded the condom. He got back to Susan's bed and enclosed her in his arms. Fulfilled and spent, the two of them fell into a quiet rest.

Susan's frightened went off at 4:00 a.m. to no one's surprise. At the point when she came to quiet the caution, she felt an arm fix around her midriff and she grinned. She ought to be depleted, yet all things considered, she was loaded up with energy. Philip had taken full advantage of the other condom a couple of hours prior. She'd woken to the vibe of his hard rooster on her posterior as he kissed and snacked his direction across her neck and back. He'd had intercourse to her like that, squeezing her alveolar with one hand while delicately stroking her clit with the other as he slid all through her.

She took a gander at Philip, with his disheveled hair and provocative, languid eyes, and grinned.

"Hello. I will wash up before I head to the cafe. It's initial. Return to rest."

She carried up and immediately strolled to the restroom. Attractive time toward the beginning of today would have been great. However, they were out of condoms and on the off chance that she didn't hustle, she'd be late. After fifteen minutes, washed, dried, and dressed, she unobtrusively opened the restroom entryway so she wouldn't upset Philip, yet acknowledged he wasn't in the bed. She tracked down him in the kitchen, pouring them both some espresso. He remained at the counter, with no shirt and an old sets of cotton rest pants that rode delectably low on his hips, displaying the little path of dim hair from his navel to his — and her — blissful spot. Out of the blue, she was enticed to phone in wiped out so she could remain in bed with Philip day in and day out.

Philip gave her a steaming mug of espresso. "I realize you have heaps of espresso at the cafe, yet I figured you could like a cup before you go."

She took a taste and grinned. "Much obliged to you. I don't ordinarily set aside some margin to brew any before I leave, yet this was exactly the very thing I wanted today."

He inclined down and gave her a waiting kiss. "Since I don't have another condom, you'll need to manage with espresso."

Philip chuckled. "I would have been so behind schedule for work." She drank the last swallow of espresso and afterward said, "Goodness, I practically neglected." She glanced through one of the kitchen drawers and found her extra house key. "Here is a key to the secondary passage. You don't have to hold on until I'm home to come in."

He took the key and stashed it. "Much thanks to you. Most days, however, I'm certain you'll be here before me."

Susan gave Philip a little kiss on the lips. "Must run. I'll see you later."

She saw that Philip remained at the secondary passage until she drove away. That just made her need to pivot and return inside. Then, at that point, she gave careful consideration to go by the drug store just after work today.

The day was occupied with bunches of clients coming in either previously or after their journey for shopping deals. Others came in for lunch looking for some different option from turkey and extras. Carly halted in for a speedy visit, and Susan educated her regarding the previous evening with Philip. Carly needed the full scoop, yet there were such a large number of clients to have that sort of discussion. She vowed to call Susan later to get every one of the subtleties.

After Susan quit for the day the day, she made the fundamental excursion to the drug store and afterward the short commute home. She dealt with a few housework and added some last enriching contacts. Her telephone rang similarly as she started contemplating what to get ready for supper. She replied and advanced toward the parlor to settle in since this planned to take some time.

"Alright, spill. I need to be aware of everything, beginning with the previous evening," was Carly's hello.

Susan discussed her proposal to allow Philip to remain with her until he could securely remain at his own home, and afterward she educated her companion concerning the previous evening. "I don't have the foggiest idea what we're doing here. We haven't exactly discussed anything explicit. However, it just felt so right to be with him, you know? Thus, I've chosen to simply accept things." Really brought a snicker from Carly.

Carly made a sound as if to speak and afterward said, "On a serious note, you should watch out. You're not made like me. You don't have it in you to be content with only an excursion. You have cheerfully at any point after composed all over you."

Susan knew precisely why Carly kept away from committed relationships. It made her extremely upset. However, Carly was correct around a certain something. Susan had never been the affection em and leave em type and she didn't think she planned to begin now. She'd simply must have some confidence in Philip. She accepted he was a decent man and she needed to invest some energy with him so he could demonstrate it. A few couples had the option to make the far-removed relationship thing work. In the event that she needed to pick between at no point ever seeing Philip in the future and just seeing him on a part time premise, she'd take what she could get at this moment. Here and there, these things had approaches to working out all alone.

"I'm about to keep a receptive outlook and an open heart and see what occurs. I continue to contemplate how things might have been if…if he hadn't needed to leave. What's more, I believe should give my very best for check whether we can get it going now." Hannah had no hesitations about her choice by any means. Love was not without chance and penance. They'd currently both forfeited the most recent seven years. So presently, she'd face a challenge.

"You realize I'll uphold you in anything choice you make. I truly trust both of you can make it work. You all were generally so wonderful together. I believe everything will be okay. Goodness, I nearly neglected to ask how your secondary school understudy is doing. You know, the one you discovered taking some time back? I have his younger sibling in my group and I realize the guardians were sincerely attempting to manage his issues."

Susan murmured. "I truly figured I could trust him. In any case, truly? I trust nothing that comes out his mouth. He truly didn't go about like he was sorry by any stretch of the imagination. Contrary to what I might think is best, I allowed him a subsequent opportunity. Be that as it may, I don't believe it will end up actually working. I'm about to let him know tomorrow that I can't move beyond what he did and he'll need to go. It'll simply be an enormous help to have him gone as of now. I can't imagine any longer that all is well."

Susan stopped when she heard her thought process was the secondary passage shutting. At the point when she didn't see Philip, she shrugged to herself, put the sound on the breeze outside and continued her discussion with Carly. "In this way,

I realize you have plans for the end of the week. Spill."

Nine

Chapter 9

Philip opened the secondary passage of Susan's home and heard her voice. Since there weren't some other vehicles in the carport, he accepted she was on the telephone. Not having any desire to upset her, he shut the entryway discreetly. As he strolled through the kitchen, he saw her sitting on the sofa and, as he suspected, she was chatting on her telephone. Be that as it may, the words he heard next left him speechless.

"I truly figured I could trust him. In any case, truly? I trust nothing that comes out his mouth. He truly didn't go about like he was sorry by any stretch of the imagination. Contrary to what I would usually prefer, I allowed him a subsequent opportunity. In any case, I don't believe it will end up actually working. I'm about to let him know tomorrow that I can't move beyond what he did and he'll need to go. It'll simply be an immense help to have him gone as of now. I can't imagine any longer that all is well."

He realized it was a chicken crap thing to do, however he pivoted, shut the entryway delicately and got back in his truck. It was only after he was out on the interstate heading toward Houston that he even started to attempt to get a handle on what he'd recently heard.

Years on the police power and he hadn't gotten on Susan's actual aims? Jesus. Furthermore, precisely what were her actual goals? Perhaps she'd simply needed to scratch a tingle. Perhaps she'd maintained that him should think everything was great between them before she reassessed. Perhaps he was slipping.

Say thanks to God he hadn't enlightened her regarding Charlie's deal some time back. He'd really been giving the chance some genuine thought of late and had wanted to converse with Susan about it this week. On the off chance that things had kept on advancing between them, he'd have been eager to think about such a move. Basically he figured out at this point. Before he'd flipped around as long as he can remember.

Notwithstanding these "silver linings," Philip was all the while stinging from the dismissal. He'd been putting it all out on the table, however evidently she'd been stabbing him in the back. For hell's sake, he didn't think he had it in him right now to keep chipping away at the house. The plan to redesign the house and keep it was, he owned up to himself, simply a reason to get back to Honey Springs so he could invest more energy with Susan.

He'd return home. Recuperate and perhaps invest some energy with Ryan before he checked with the chief about pulling out his get-away solicitation. No real reason for simply lounging around for the following five weeks. Fortunately, he'd secured his home for the night. His instruments and hardware were still inside. He didn't figure anybody would irritate any of it, however he'd call Charlie and request that he watch out for things there.

"Sheriff Weaver," Charlie replied after a couple of rings.

"Hello, Charlie, it's Philip. See, I was expecting to request some help. I'm going to Houston and I would truly see the value in it in the event that you could watch out for the house for some time."

"Indeed, Philip. That is no issue. I'll make certain to remember it for the customary rounds. Something' happen that you're returning to Houston so out of nowhere?"

Philip had zero desire to let anybody know that he'd been misdirected. "Actually no, not actually. I just chose with Christmas coming up that it would be smarter to be home." Approach, Philip. Might you at some point make up much else faltering? I have to strongly disagree.

From the quiet on the opposite finish of the telephone, he'd say Charlie wasn't succumbing to his reason. "I see," Charlie at long last said. "I, er, thought perhaps you and Susan were reuniting. I'd heard a few things and — "

"Well," said Philip, "I'd believed that as well. However, that is not in the cards now."

Charlie's reaction verged on irate. "I genuinely trust you didn't play Susan for a fast rush."

Philip woofed out a cruel snicker. "As a matter of fact, I assume I was the person who got played."

Charlie breathed out noisily and said, "Now that doesn't seem like Susan by any means."

"No offense, man, however I won't examine what happened among me and Susan. I'll simply say it won't work. Presently, all things considered, I haven't concluded how I will manage it yet. It's been sitting up for quite a while, so somewhat longer won't do any harm. I left a portion of my things in there. In the event that you could simply watch out on the spot, I'd see the value in it."

"I'll ensure the house is secure and watch out for things." Charlie stopped like he didn't know how to proceed. "You realize my entryway is generally open to talk."

Philip took a quieting breath and said, "Much obliged. That's what I value." No chance I will hold nothing back to Charlie Weaver.

Regrettably, Charlie made a sound as if to speak and said, "You know, when I'd heard a few discussion about you and Susan conceivably reuniting, I thought perhaps you'd give a serious thought to my proposal about the sheriff's situation."

"I value your confidence and trust in me. I truly do. However, I don't believe that will work out either." Which annoyed Philip since he'd really contemplated the conceivable outcomes.

"For hell's sake, I figured it would be an ideal answer for the two of us. In any case, who knows. Perhaps you'll have the option to sort out things ultimately. At any rate, I wasn't in a genuine rush to leave right now."

Frantic to get the other man off the telephone, Philip said, "I'll inform you as to whether anything changes and when I hope to be back in the neighborhood. In the case of anything occurs, you can contact me at this number."

"I'll stay in contact. Converse with you soon, Philip."

Philip disengaged the call and turned on the radio, expecting to lose himself in the exemplary stone melodies. No such karma. All things considered, he thought about how Charlie might have realized that he and Susan had been…seeing one another. Then, at that point, he recollected that it was Honey Springs and that was exactly the way in which the town worked. It would have been great assuming somebody had enlightened him concerning Susan's goals.

Except for a couple of stops for fuel and food, Philip passed straight through and shown up at his condo around 12 PM. He was bone tired. He'd worked the entire day at his home and afterward left to go to Susan's. Poo. Appeared to be a lifetime prior at this point. Without turning on any lights, he strolled to his room, stripped down to his fighters and fell into bed. He was depleted and ought to have nodded off immediately. In any case, Susan's voice, so matter of reality and cool, continued to reverberate in his mind. Contrary to what he would usually prefer, he saw his telephone. He had around ten missed calls and two times that number of instant messages. Also, three voice message messages. All from Susan.

He squeezed play and heard Susan's voice, sweet and hot, asking where he was on the grounds that time was slipping away. In the following message, she sounded more concerned yet probably accepted he was all the while working at his home. The last message made his heart hurt.

"Philip? I don't see the reason why you won't call me. Is an off-base thing? I just went to your home and you weren't there. Everything was secured. Did your companion begin having intricacies? If it's not too much trouble, simply call me and let me in on you're OK. If it's not too much trouble."

Presently, he didn't have any idea what to think. She seemed like the old Susan. His Susan. Is it safe to say that she was simply vexed on the grounds that she didn't get to advise him to screw off like she arranged? Genuinely and sincerely depleted, he switched off his telephone and fell into a forlorn rest, with dreams of Susan and his dad.

He came alert promptly with the beating on his entryway. His clock read 9:00 a.m. Who the fuck was beating on his entryway? Without really thinking, he snatched his mm from the bedside cabinet, pulled on a couple of running pants and strolled to the entryway. He assumed he was seeing things when he glanced through the peephole. He opened the entryway and investigated Susan's angry eyes.

When the entryway opened and Susan saw Philip, the main feeling she felt was alleviation. And afterward, she blew up. In the event that she wasn't on a profound thrill ride for the beyond eight hours, she would have thought the befuddled and amazed demeanor all over was entertaining. Perhaps later, she'd giggle about it, yet not presently. Presently, she was scarcely maintaining a level of control, and that work was being upheld by her outrage. So she would clutch that and brave this. She'd never been the kind of individual who loved struggle or conflict. Be that as it may, today, she'd make a special case.

"Susan!" said Philip.

"You bastard!" expressed Susan with scarcely controlled fierceness. "How dare you," she proceeded.
  "Susan!" said Philip.

"You bastard!" expressed Susan with scarcely controlled wrath. "How dare you," she proceeded.

"Susan," Philip rehashed. "What are you doing here?"

"I'm doing what I ought to have completed a long time back, you charlatan."

Before Philip could answer, he saw a few neighbors had made

their ways for see what was going on with the uproar. He glanced back at Susan. "For what reason don't we head inside so we can talk in private?"

Susan squinted her eyes. "Talk? You need to talk now? For what reason didn't you think of this quite astute thought, well, I don't know…eight hours prior?" Her voice had gotten logically stronger with each word.

Presently, a few of the neighbors were transparently inquisitive and effectively tuning in. Susan truly couldn't have cared less on the off chance that she humiliated Philip, however this wasn't a discussion she needed to have with a group of people.

She followed him inside his loft and held back when she saw the weapon in his grasp. The fact that he had his weapon makes her stunned. He was a regulation official and she had been beating on his entryway like a battering ram. However, she was unable to help her sarcastic comment. "I might be truly annoyed, yet I'm no risk to you, so could you lose the weapon?"

Philip peered down at his hand and recollected he was all the while holding it. He turned and passed on the kitchen to take care of it back. Susan made a move to glance around. She didn't know what she'd expected, yet the truth of Philip's loft was just…well, it was simply miserable. She saw no photos or individual things. It seemed like he'd recently moved in. Perhaps he had. However, she thought not. Other than the couple he discussed who had encouraged him when he initially got to Houston, he truly had no family. He'd never referenced any aunties or uncles on either his mom's or alternately father's side.

Philip returned and her pondering finished. Before she continued her past condition of frantic, she paused for a minute to grieve the way that while Philip was out of the room, he'd gotten some margin to get into a shirt. Hell. On the off chance that this would have been her last standoff with the man, the least he might have done was give her something to check out. So that made her distraught, as well.

He went directly to one of the above cupboards and took out a canister and afterward start filling the espresso pot with water. "I could truly utilize some espresso. What about you?"

Her eyes felt like sandpaper each time she flickered, and she had a pressure cerebral pain. Espresso sounded magnificent. "Certainly."

"I have no nourishment for breakfast. I didn't plan..." Hannah thought he quit talking mid sentence since he would have rather not examined that subject at this moment.

Indeed, that was simply too damn terrible in light of the fact that she did. However, she incredibly required some espresso first.

They stayed there, depleted and red-looked at, gazing at one another. The hints of murmuring and water dribbling appeared to be enhanced in the minuscule kitchen.

"What are you doing here?" Philip asked once more.

Obviously, he wouldn't trust that the espresso will start. She'd add that to her rundown of motivations to be distraught.

"What's your arrangement?" Should simply bounce on in, thought Susan..

Philip glared. "What's my arrangement? What in the world does that mean?"

Unfathomable. "Truly? You have no clue about what I'm referring to?"

"Not a sign." His response was short and…angry?

Despite her desire to the contrary, she felt tears accumulate in her eyes, yet she'd be cursed assuming she'd allow them to fall. She flickered quickly a couple of times to gather them up. "I'm discussing your arrangement of leaving. Is this something you do to all ladies? Or on the other hand am I simply extraordinary like that?"

Philip squinted his eyes yet said nothing. All things being equal, he got up and poured them both some espresso. He opened the bureau once more and tracked down sugar and powdered flavor. He added a liberal sum into Susan's cup and afterward offered the two cups that would be useful and gotten back to his seat. Neither talked while they took mindful tastes of the hot, superb fluid.

In the wake of drinking a large portion of his espresso, he put the cup down and fixed her with a virus gaze. "I've made sense of and apologized for the initial twice I needed to leave you. In any case, I'll be doomed assuming I'll apologize for leaving the previous evening and denying you of the joy of dismissing me. You needed to get rid of me. So I left. For what reason you're here at this point? I don't have a fucking hint."

Susan shifted her head aside while she attempted to translate Philip's words. Did he simply say he left before she could advise him to leave? Or on the other hand would he say he was curving things around to make him seem to be the person in question?

"I have no clue about what you're referring to. How could you think I needed to get over you?"

Philip raised one doubtful eyebrow. "You don't need to lie, Susan. I heard you."

Susan scowled and shook her head, confounded.

With a moan, Philip reclined and said, "OK. If that is the manner in which you need to play this, I'll come. At the point when I strolled in the secondary passage the previous evening, I heard you chatting on the telephone. I heard you say you were unable to believe me and you accepted nothing I said. That you allowed me a subsequent opportunity however it wasn't actually working. You said you planned to let me know the following day that it simply wasn't actually working and it would be a help whenever I was gone and you wouldn't need to imagine any longer."

Susan was both sickened and alleviated when she understood precisely very thing he'd heard. "Gracious, Philip. You fail to understand the situation." Before Philip could protest, she proceeded. "I was conversing with Carly and enlightening her regarding one of the great school understudies who worked for me that was found taking. After a gathering with his folks and school authorities, I allowed him a subsequent opportunity, yet it simply wasn't actually working. You heard that."

"You were discussing a worker," Philip said bluntly, nearly to himself.

"Indeed, truth be told. I fail to see the reason why you'd figure I would agree that those things about you, particularly after the prior night. I thought we planned to push ahead, invest more energy together…remember every one of the reasons we fell head over heels previously." She wouldn't be humiliated about what was in her heart.

Philip sat back in his seat and cleaned his without a doubt his face. "I don't have any idea why I rushed to think you were discussing me." He stopped and peered down briefly. "Perhaps I didn't really accept that you could genuinely pardon me. Perhaps I need more confidence in myself to accept I truly deserve your absolution."

Hearing Philip concede this about himself was appalling. She chose at that moment to do everything within her power to persuade this man he deserved pardoning and love.

She stood and strolled around to him. In one smooth movement, she swung her leg across his lap to ride him. Grasping his face, she said, "You are not your dad. You weren't in those days and you're not presently. You are meriting adoration and pardoning."

And afterward, in light of the fact that she was unable to help herself, she squeezed her lips to his for a sweet, delicate kiss. She moved back and trusted that his eyes will open. At the point when they did, and she saw such a lot of affection and satisfaction sparkling there, she folded her arms over his neck and afterward kissed him hard. She felt his arms come around her and crush her firmly to his chest. His kisses turned out to be more enthusiastic and serious and she could feel his erection at her center. As her craving developed, she moved her hips against his hardness which just increased her need. Then, at that point, she felt his hands go to her butt and he rose from the seat. Never lifting his mouth from hers, he strolled them to his room.

As they tumbled onto the bed, Philip chose top of her and carried his hands to her face. "I need you," he murmured.

Susan grinned as she turned her head to kiss the center of his hand. "I'm yours."

Philip's heart skirted a thump. He couldn't say whether she implied in a real sense or only until further notice. One way or another, he'd take it. Since he'd had a brief look into a world without Susan now. It was not where he needed to be. Thus, he'd acknowledge anything she was ready to give and afterward trust he could persuade her to need more. He didn't figure he ought to say the words at the present time, yet he could damn well show her how he felt.

He constrained himself to dial back. He needed to take as much time as necessary, form the longing between them until it consumed hot and splendid. The main errand, however, was to get her bare. Running his hands along the fix of her Shirt, he said, "We should get these garments off."

"Stand by," Susan said, her hand preventing his from pulling up her shirt.

Philip gulped hard and inquired, "What's going on here? Would you like to stop?" God, please. That's what everything except.

"You have condoms, correct? If it's not too much trouble, say you have condoms," Susan asked direly.

Briefly, Philip's psyche went clear. They'd utilized the condoms he'd put away in his wallet. His restless and want filled mind battled to plainly think. Then, at that point, he grinned, opened the cabinet of the end table and figured out how to find one solitary condom bundle. He held it up victoriously.

Susan looked frustrated and inquired, "You just have one?"

Philip arrived at down and pulled Susan's shirt over her head and afterward eliminated her bra. Fast work was made of eliminating her pants and undies too. Philip settled down on Susan, bowed his head and licked her bosom, grinning as he watched the alveolar solidify. "I guarantee you, child. I'll make the most of that one condom."

With that, Susan angled her back so her bosoms were pushed

nearer to his mouth. "You like it when I suck on these pink alveolars, don't you?" Not hanging tight for a response, he licked one of her alveolars, prodding it with his tongue, until he brought it into his mouth and started to suck in profound musical pulls.

Susan answered by groaning and pulling his head closer to her bosom as she raised her hips to draw nearer to his chicken, which was taking steps to break liberated from the bounds of his warm up pants. Jesus. Susan's reaction to his lovemaking had forever been similar to tossing a match onto fuel. The two of them disintegrated and afterward wore wild. It had been that way when they were youthful and it was that way now. He needed just to detach his garments and sink balls profound into her. And keeping in mind that that could exhibit exactly how insane with want he became when he was with her, it wouldn't tell her that she was so valuable to him. Along these lines, he kept adoring her bosoms and bit by bit kissed his direction down her body until, finally, he was at her pussy.

He ran a finger through the delicate blonde twists to stroke her clit daintily. At the point when her hips started to buck, he put his hand across her gut to keep her still, his thumb delicately getting across her delicate skin. "Unwind, child. I have you," Philip murmured. And afterward, on the grounds that he just couldn't stand by one more second longer, he brought down his head and licked at her delicate, wet folds.

Hearing her sharp admission of breath, he grinned to himself as he carried two gives over to open her up more completely to his mouth. He proceeded to lick and suck as her cries and requests for more became stronger. Before both of them could fall over that euphoric edge, Philip immediately shucked off his running pants and moved on the condom. At the point when he was ready over her, her eyes were shut and she was moving her head to and fro, ambiguous words coming from her lips.

"Susan, take a gander at me," he murmured.

She stilled and opened her eyes at his solicitation. God. However long he lived, he'd recollect her at this time. So amazingly gorgeous. Eyes coated with want. "I'm finished leaving you." He gradually sank into her body, his eyes never leaving hers. "I'm staying put."

Ten

Chapter 10

Susan laid her head on Philip's chest while she sat tight for her breathing to get back to business as usual. The consistent all over development of her head told her Philip was likewise battling to pause and rest. She felt like her body was weighted down, and she scarcely had the energy to squint her eyes. Without getting her head, she said lethargically, "You were correct."

It seemed Philip needed to call the energy to answer. "Really? About what?"

"You said you'd make the most of that one condom. Job well done, sir." Susan figured out how to lift her head and wink at Philip. She laid her head down and said, "I'm happy I didn't convince myself not to drive around here to stand up to you."

Philip got the additional pad and put it under his head so he was leaning back more against the headboard. Susan had hurried forward so her head might in any case lay on his chest. Philip said, "I needed to get some information about that. How could you know where to track down me? Or on the other hand even that I'd return home?"

Susan inactively ran her fingers through the sprinkling of hair on Philip's chest. "From the start, when you didn't return home, I thought perhaps you'd been postponed or had chosen to go visit somebody. However at that point after I continued calling and not finding a solution, I got stressed. I started to believe that perhaps you'd hurt yourself some way or another at your home and couldn't answer the telephone."

Philip's arm fixed around her, as though to show his lament at making her concern.

"After I went out to the house and saw that nobody was there, I had returned to accepting you'd got together with somebody for a little while and perhaps your telephone was dead. Be that as it may, the later it got, the more stressed I became. I at last called Charlie and let him know I thought something had happened to you. Furthermore, that is the point at which he made sense of that you'd return to Houston. I persuaded him to give me your location. I nearly worked myself out of it, however at that point I just got in my vehicle, set the GPS, and I'm right here."

Philip kissed her delicately on the head. "I'm truly happy you didn't pay attention to consistent Susan. However, what had the effect this time?"

Susan created some distance from her situation on Philip's chest and sat with folded legs close to him. "At the point when you left quite a while back without a word, I didn't actually attempt to track down you. Or on the other hand figure out why you left. I rushed to accept you'd concluded you needed some other person or thing. And afterward, when you needed to pass on to go see about your accomplice, my response was something similar. I was harmed and furious, yet I didn't search for you. Or on the other hand for replies. I didn't battle for you."

She truly preferred not to say this. She realized it was valid, yet it was simply so difficult to acknowledge. She hadn't battled for Philip. Somebody she'd maintained to adore. Furthermore, she hadn't battled for him. What did that say regarding her?

With certifiable lament, Susan said, "Please accept my apologies I didn't battle for you. I ought to have."

Philip sat up and went after Susan. "Kindly don't do that to yourself. We were both youthful and did all that could be expected."

Susan grinned tragically. "I realize you're correct. However, I'm not that youthful high school young lady any longer. So the previous evening, after I'd precluded that you were harmed some place, I simply didn't have any desire to accept that you'd done it to me once more. Also, not set in stone to defy you and let you know — " She halted, as though she understood what she was going to say. Obviously, Philip called her on it.

"Tell me what?"

"Not entirely set in stone to tell you that this time, I planned to battle for you." She chomped her lip and grinned waywardly. "All things considered, I planned to battle for you after I gave my opinion."

Philip laughed at that. "You were surely spitting frantic when I opened the entryway."

"I'm happy I came here," Susan said, her voice temperamental. Not entirely settled to investigate every possibility, she inquired, "Were you serious about your previous statement? About not leaving once more?"

Philip's face became serious as he delicately pushed her back and followed her down on the bed. Scouring his nose along hers, he said, "I stood by everything there."

"Along these lines, what you're talking about is you need to go consistent?" Susan prodded.

Philip's eyes were grinning and loaded up with warmth and love. "That is precisely exact thing I'm saying."

Susan folded her arms over Philip's neck and said, "I'm willing to attempt the significant distance-relationship thing."

Philip delayed the slightest bit and afterward said, "There may be a way for us to be together. Nothing is permanently established at this moment, but…Charlie Weaver inquired as to whether I would be keen on assuming control over his situation as sheriff once he resigns. I've been giving it some serious idea."

Susan was torn between joy at the chance of having the option to accompany Philip consistently, and culpability that he'd need to relinquish his position and home.

"I can't request that you surrender your life here for me. You ought not be the main one to forfeit so we can be together."

Philip shook his head. "No. The genuine penance would be not having the option to see you consistently or rest next to you consistently. Furthermore, subsequent to seeing what befell Ryan, I've been contemplating rolling out certain improvements in my day to day existence. What's more, in the event that those changes bring us closer, I'm in with no reservations. That is no penance by any means."

Still uncomfortable with Philip totally evacuating his life for her, she said, "Commitment me you'll get every one of the subtleties before you do anything intense. Well, you need to come to no snap conclusions about this or be in a rush. I'm staying put."

He kissed her daintily and afterward said, "I vow to consult with Charlie about the subtleties of the gig. Presently, could we go out for breakfast since I have no food here."

"I'd like that," Susan said. "I'm starving."

Sunday morning, Philip strolled Susan to her vehicle and kissed her long and hard. He realized it was sappy, yet he would have rather not let her go. Also, that main supported his choice to take the action to Honey Springs. For hell's sake, with the manner in which he felt now, on the off chance that the sheriff position didn't work out, perhaps he'd wash dishes at Susan's bistro. He wouldn't lose her once more.

He was unable to recall the last time he'd felt so cheerful and content. As a matter of fact, now that he'd mulled over everything, he hadn't felt as such since secondary school. He'd never encountered these equivalent feelings with some other lady. What's more, he didn't think he at any point would. Also, if feeling as such implied he needed to turn in his man card, all things considered, so be it.

Recently, they'd gone for breakfast and afterward giggled and talked and made love the remainder of the day and a large portion of the evening. Top on the need list after breakfast was loading up on condoms. Fortunately, he'd purchased the biggest box that anyone could hope to find.

He'd been allowed a second opportunity with Susan, and he wouldn't mess it up once more. In the wake of finishing the kiss, he folded his arms over her and embraced her tight. "Call me frequently so I realize you're OK. Furthermore, let me know when you return home."

She gestured and said, "I will."

Hesitantly, he pulled away and opened her vehicle entryway. Subsequent to aiding her inside, he shut the entryway and inclined down to give her another light kiss. "I'll see you soon."

As he watched her drive away, it felt like his heart would leap out of his chest. He knew. Without a tiny trace of uncertainty. He planned to wed that lady.

At the point when he strolled once again into his condo, it appeared to be considerably more exposed and forsaken than it had been previously. No real reason for transforming anything now since he didn't want to be there significantly longer.

Usually on Sundays, he'd go work out and afterward observe a few games on television. In any case, presently, he felt fretful. It was like he was prepared to set each of his issues up so he could move to Honey Springs.

He wouldn't have the option to place in his notification at the station until tomorrow, yet he expected to converse with Ryan about it first. In the wake of messaging Ryan to ensure this was a great opportunity to come around, Philip traveled that way.

Despite the fact that Ryan had been released from the clinic, he actually had a long recuperation in front of him. Since he needed some everyday support, and he didn't have a spouse or consistent sweetheart, he'd had no real option except to move in with his twin sister, Rayleigh. This was really his most ideal choice since Rayleigh was a medical caretaker. Truly, she was a pediatric medical caretaker, yet she was more than equipped for checking Ryan's recovery.

Philip showed up at Rayleigh's loft about an hour after the fact, conveying a container of still-warm-from-the-broiler doughnuts. Rayleigh grinned when she opened the entryway.

"Philip," she said. "Seeing you is great. Furthermore, you brought doughnuts, I see! Kindly, if it's not too much trouble, kindly let me know there's one jam filled?" She checked out ideally at the case in Philip's grasp.

Philip folded his free arm over Rayleigh's midriff and gave her a fast kiss on the cheek. "No," Philip said truly and grinned when he saw her disheartened articulation. "There's two," he said conceitedly and was compensated with another splendid grin.

Rayleigh remained back and motioned for Philip to enter. "Enter," she said. "Ryan's in the family room."

Philip followed Rayleigh and really wanted to see the swing of her hips as she strolled. For sure. She was a delightful lady, with liberal bends and an incredible character. She was thoughtful and shrewd and lovely. Furthermore, Philip felt literally nothing when he was close to her. Be that as it may, simply contemplating Susan could make him hard as a stone. He guessed that was the way it ought to be.

Ryan was in a chair in the family room writing in a scratch pad when Philip strolled in. Philip was feeling quite a bit better to see his companion looking so well. He had a cast on his leg and he must be mindful so as not to upset the lines on his mid-region and side, however his tone was great, regardless of whether his perspective was not. At first, after he was shot, his emphasis was on making due. At the point when he crossed that obstacle and started to gain proficiency with the degree of his wounds and the drawn out impacts, he was confronted with an obscure future in policing. It was far fetched his leg would be completely useful since one of the projectiles broke his femur. It was normal that his inner wounds would ultimately recuperate totally, however it would be a long interaction.

Crap. Philip hadn't pondered what his news could mean for his companion. Ryan was managing a ton, and Mack nearly felt like he'd focus on his satisfaction Ryan's face. Ryan gazed upward from his note pad and grinned.

"Hello, man," Ryan said. Subsequent to looking at the container in Philip's grasp, he proceeded, "And I see you brought breakfast. Decent." Ryan arrived at in the container and eliminated a frosted doughnut. Rayleigh showed up abruptly and culled the two jam finished circles of bliss up of the crate.

"Simply moving these." Rayleigh took a chomp from one preceding she strolled back to the kitchen. "I'm making espresso. I'll bring some out when it's prepared."

Philip sat on the sofa and checked his companion out. "At any rate, I know it's the standard inquiry, however I'll ask. How goes it with you?"

Ryan shrugged and expressed, "Sucks to need to depend on your sister to assist you with getting around. Sucks to be trapped in this loft day in and day out. Sucks to realize I won't ever return to the region." He peered down briefly and afterward thought back up to Philip. "In any case, it would suck more to be dead. In this way, I'll simply take it each day in turn for the present."

Philip had thought Ryan wouldn't have the option to get back to police work, yet hearing him express it without holding back truly pounded it home. "Perhaps, in the event that you give it sufficient opportunity — "

"All the time on the planet won't recover the bone in my leg. Also, I'm truly not keen on rearranging papers there while the genuine police go back and forth." Ryan investigated at the note pad he'd been writing in when Philip showed up. "I was the third era of police in my loved ones. I've seen and heard a ton of things throughout the long term. I've been playing with utilizing those accounts and encounters to compose fiction spine chillers. For hell's sake, dislike a have very little time to burn at this moment."

As Philip took a decent, hard gander at Ryan, he said a glimmer of energy in his eyes when he discussed composition. "I feel that is really smart, man." Philip smiled and proceeded, "dislike you will not have a lot of material to work with."

Ryan appeared to be freed to hear Philip's approval from his thought for a future beyond the police division. "Anyway, did you just come to convey doughnuts, or was there one more explanation you dropped by?"

Philip intellectually shook his head. Ryan was both keen and direct.

"I, uh, needed to tell you I intend to leave the office and move to Honey Springs. Most likely before the year's end."

Ryan shifted his head and said, "Brother, this isn't brand new information to me. You're moving to be close to your lady."

Philip couldn't conceal his shock. "How did you — "

"Man. Truly? In the years we've known one another, you've never discussed any lady. Presently, since you reconnected with Susan after your father's administrations, she's all you've discussed. You have another opportunity currently so don't mess it up. Also, to make things abundantly clear, I would have let you know exactly the same thing in the event that I wasn't confronting a few significant changes myself."

Feeling like an enormous stone had quite recently been taken off his mind, he proceeded to enlighten Ryan concerning his arrangements. He was one bit nearer now and couldn't stand by to cross the end goal.

It was Christmas eve and Susan had recently filled two mugs with thick, rich hot cocoa. As she conveyed the mugs into the front room, she needed to pause and squeeze herself at the prospect of what was currently her life. Philip had spread a blanket on the floor before the chimney and was loosened up there, his back facing the sofa. He turned upward when she entered and the articulation in his eyes she'd become acquainted with seeing. Warmth. Appreciation. Love.

In the weeks since his return, they'd went through each night together. He kept on chipping away at his home yet had no particular designs for how to manage it whenever it was finished. Charlie's arrangements went off easily. Charlie resigned and Philip was designated by the town gathering as sheriff. Susan presently not questioned Philip's capacity and want to remain. They'd both presented the "L" word to one another after an especially delicate lovemaking meeting not long after his move back. She cherished this man with a curiousness she hadn't thought she was able to do. Cherishing him as a young person had quite recently been a hint of something larger. Furthermore, realizing he felt the same way? Beyond value.

He arrived at up to take the mugs from her hands so she could plunk down on the floor also. Whenever she was settled, he gave her one of the mugs and together, they tasted and watched the flares dance around the logs in the chimney. Her heart was full and practically spilling over. Susan's folks had called to say they wouldn't be in that frame of mind on Christmas day because of dangerous driving circumstances in Colorado. She was restless to see her folks, however she was likewise grateful for the time alone with Mack.

She took a taste of her beverage and said, "I don't figure tonight could get any more great." And afterward she thought briefly. "In reality, I figure a little snow would be what might get the job done." The weather conditions gauge prior had shown a little chance of snow.

"Perhaps there's something different that would work similarly as well."

Philip set his mug on the floor and went after a case that had been covered under a cushion on the love seat.

Susan's heart halted briefly and afterward fortunately continued thumping, albeit, presently, the cadence had kicked up altogether.

Philip delicately took the mug from her hands and set it on the floor. Holding her left hand, he said, "I cherished you as a kid and afterward I needed to leave you. I love you now. As a man. Also, I guarantee that the possibly way I'll leave you again is the point at which I take my final gasp. I love you, Susan Fry. Will you marry me?"

Philip let go of Susan's hand so he could open the case and recover the ring. With a shaky grin, she took a gander at the man she cherished, and murmured, "Yes. I love you so much, Philip Brownsville."

As he slid the ring on her finger, he said, "I believed this ring should address our excursion. One stone is for our past and one is for our present. The one in the center is our future. Splendid and huge."

With bittersweet tears bliss obscuring her vision, Susan peered down at the ring on her shaking hand and saw the center stone was sparkling and sparkling with the commitment of for eternity. She folded her arms over Philip's neck and kissed him with all the affection she had in her heart. As he delicately let her down on the blanket and covered her body with his, lovely little snowflakes drifted tenderly to the ground outside.

Eleven

Also by NIKKI WEST

CAUGHT IN A LIE
AND MANY OTHER NOVEL.

Twelve

APPRECIATION

∾⋯∽

Thanks to my readers for reading my book and am remain blessed in everything you are a doing. Do well by writing a review for other readers to read and enjoy my story.